Headlong Hall by Thomas

Thomas Love Peacock was born on October 18th 1785 in Weymouth, Dorset.

His education was never completed and mainly self-taught Thomas was made a clerk with Ludlow Fraser Company, merchants in the City of London. In 1800

For Thomas life was work and the nurturing of his writing. When time allowed he would visit the Reading Room of the British Museum to study classic literature.

In 1804 and 1806 he published two volumes of poetry, The Monks of St. Mark and Palmyra. By 1809 he has also published his great poem 'The Genius of the Thames'.

Peacock travelled to North Wales in January 1810 where he visited Maentwrog and met his future wife, Jane Gryffydh.

By September 1815 had settled at Great Marlow and wrote Headlong Hall in 1815. It was published the following year. With this work Peacock found the true field for his literary gift in the satiric novel. Peacock continued to produce; the satirical novels Melincourt in 1817 and Nightmare Abbey in 1818.

At the beginning of 1819, Peacock was summoned to London for probation with the East India Company. Peacock's test papers earned the commendation, "Nothing superfluous and nothing wanting." This career was to run alongside his literary one for several decades.

Peacock married Jane Griffith or Gryffydh in 1820. They went on to have four children.

In 1820 Peacock wrote The Four Ages of Poetry, which argued that poetry's relevance was being eclipsed by science, a claim which provoked Shelley's Defence of Poetry.

In the winter of 1825–6 he wrote Paper Money Lyrics and other Poems "during the prevalence of an influenza to which the beautiful fabric of paper-credit is periodically subject."

In 1829 he published The Misfortunes of Elphin, and in 1831 Crotchet Castle, the most mature and perhaps most appreciated of his works.

By 1836 his official career was crowned by his appointment as Chief Examiner of Indian Correspondence.

In about 1852 towards the end of Peacock's service in the India office, his taste for leisure and appetite for writing returned and with it his entertaining and scholarly Horæ Dramaticæ.

In 1860 came the publication of his last novel; Gryll Grange. Later, that same year he added the appendix of Shelley's letters, a matter of great literary importance.

Thomas Love Peacock died at Lower Halliford, on 23rd January, 1866, from injuries sustained in a fire in attempting to save his library. He is buried in the new cemetery at Shepperton.

Index of Contents

PREFACE - To "Headlong Hall" and the three novels published along with it in 1837.

All these little publications appeared originally without prefaces. I left them to speak for themselves; and I thought I might very fitly preserve my own impersonality, having never intruded on the personality of others, nor taken any liberties but with public conduct and public opinions. But an old friend assures me, that to publish a book without a preface is like entering a drawing-room without making a bow. In deference to this opinion, though I am not quite clear of its soundness, I make my prefatory bow at this eleventh hour.

"Headlong Hall" was written in 1815; "Nightmare Abbey" in 1817; "Maid Marian", with the exception of the last three chapters, in 1818; "Crotchet Castle" in 1830. I am desirous to note the intervals, because, at each of those periods, things were true, in great matters and in small, which are true no longer. "Headlong Hall" begins with the Holyhead Mail, and "Crotchet Castle" ends with a rotten borough. The Holyhead mail no longer keeps the same hours, nor stops at the Capel Cerig Inn, which the progress of improvement has thrown out of the road; and the rotten boroughs of 1830 have ceased to exist, though there are some very pretty pocket properties, which are their worthy successors. But the classes of tastes, feelings, and opinions, which were successively brought into play in these little tales, remain substantially the same. Perfectibilians, deteriorationists, statu-quo-ites, phrenologists, transcendentalists, political economists, theorists in all sciences, projectors in all arts, morbid visionaries, romantic enthusiasts, lovers of music, lovers of the picturesque, and lovers of good dinners, march, and will march for ever, pari passu with the march of mechanics, which some facetiously call the march of the intellect. The fastidious in old wine are a race that does not decay. Literary violators of the confidences of private life still gain a disreputable livelihood and an unenviable notoriety. Match-makers from interest, and the disappointed in love and in friendship, are varieties of which specimens are extant. The great principle of the Right of Might is as flourishing now as in the days of Maid Marian: the array of false pretensions, moral, political, and literary, is as imposing as ever: the rulers of the world still feel things in their effects, and never foresee them in their causes: and political mountebanks continue, and will continue, to puff nostrums and practise legerdemain under the eyes of the multitude: following, like the "learned friend" of Crotchet Castle, a course as tortuous as that of a river, but in a reverse process; beginning by being dark and deep, and ending by being transparent.

The Author of "Headlong Hall".

March 4, 1837.

Chapter I

The Mail

The ambiguous light of a December morning, peeping through the windows of the Holyhead mail, dispelled the soft visions of the four insides, who had slept, or seemed to sleep, through the first seventy miles of the road, with as much comfort as may be supposed consistent with the jolting of the vehicle, and an occasional admonition to remember the coachman, thundered through the open door, accompanied by the gentle breath of Boreas, into the ears of the drowsy traveller.

A lively remark, that the day was none of the finest, having elicited a repartee of quite the contrary, the various knotty points of meteorology, which usually form the exordium of an English conversation, were successively discussed and exhausted; and, the ice being thus broken, the colloquy rambled to other topics, in the course of which it appeared, to the surprise of every one, that all four, though perfect strangers to each other, were actually bound to the same point, namely, Headlong Hall, the seat of the ancient and honourable family of the Headlongs, of the vale of Llanberris, in Caernarvonshire. This name may appear at first sight not to be truly Cambrian, like those of the Rices, and Prices, and Morgans, and Owens, and Williamses, and Evanses, and Parrys, and Joneses; but, nevertheless, the Headlongs claim to be not less genuine derivatives from the antique branch of Cadwallader than any of the last named multiramified families. They claim, indeed, by one account, superior antiquity to all of them, and even to Cadwallader himself, a tradition having been handed down in Headlong Hall for some few thousand years, that the founder of the family was preserved in the deluge on the summit of Snowdon, and took the name of Rhaiader, which signifies a waterfall, in consequence of his having accompanied the water in its descent or diminution, till he found himself comfortably seated on the rocks of Llanberris. But, in later days, when commercial bagmen began to scour the country, the ambiguity of the sound induced his descendants to drop the suspicious denomination of Riders, and translate the word into English; when, not being well pleased with the sound of the thing, they substituted that of the quality, and accordingly adopted the name Headlong, the appropriate epithet of waterfall.

I cannot tell how the truth may be: I say the tale as 'twas said to me.

The present representative of this ancient and dignified house, Harry Headlong, Esquire, was, like all other Welsh squires, fond of shooting, hunting, racing, drinking, and other such innocent amusements, meizonos d' allou tinos, as Menander expresses it. But, unlike other Welsh squires, he had actually suffered certain phenomena, called books, to find their way into his house; and, by dint of lounging over them after dinner, on those occasions when he was compelled to take his bottle alone, he became seized with a violent passion to be thought a philosopher and a man of taste; and accordingly set off on an expedition to Oxford, to inquire for other varieties of the same genera, namely, men of taste and philosophers; but, being assured by a learned professor that there were no such things in the University, he proceeded to London, where, after beating up in several booksellers' shops, theatres, exhibition-rooms, and other resorts of literature and taste, he formed as extensive an acquaintance with philosophers and dilettanti as his utmost ambition could desire: and it now became his chief wish to have them all together in Headlong Hall, arguing, over his old Port and Burgundy, the various knotty points which had puzzled his pericranium. He had, therefore, sent them invitations in due form to pass their Christmas at Headlong Hall; which invitations the extensive fame of his kitchen fire had induced the greater part of them to accept; and four of the chosen guests had, from different parts of the metropolis, ensconced themselves in the four corners of the Holyhead mail.

These four persons were, Mr Foster[1.1], the perfectibilian; Mr Escot[1.2], the deteriorationist; Mr Jenkison[1.3], the statu-quo-ite; and the Reverend Doctor Gaster[1.4], who, though of course neither a philosopher nor a man of taste, had so won on the Squire's fancy, by a learned dissertation on the art of stuffing a turkey, that he concluded no Christmas party would be complete without him.

The conversation among these illuminati soon became animated; and Mr Foster, who, we must observe, was a thin gentleman, about thirty years of age, with an aquiline nose, black eyes, white teeth, and black hair,took occasion to panegyrize the vehicle in which they were then travelling, and observed what remarkable improvements had been made in the means of facilitating intercourse between distant parts of the kingdom: he held forth with great energy on the subject of roads and railways, canals and tunnels, manufactures and machinery: "In short," said he, "everything we look on attests the progress of mankind in all the arts of life, and demonstrates their gradual advancement towards a state of unlimited perfection."

Mr Escot, who was somewhat younger than Mr Foster, but rather more pale and saturnine in his aspect, here took up the thread of the discourse, observing, that the proposition just advanced seemed to him perfectly contrary to the true state of the case: "for," said he, "these improvements, as you call them, appear to me only so many links in the great chain of corruption, which will soon fetter the whole human race in irreparable slavery and incurable wretchedness: your improvements proceed in a simple ratio, while the factitious wants and unnatural appetites they engender proceed in a compound one; and thus one generation acquires fifty wants, and fifty means of supplying them are invented, which each in its turn engenders two new ones; so that the next generation has a hundred, the next two hundred, the next four hundred, till every human being becomes such a helpless compound of perverted inclinations, that he is altogether at the mercy of external circumstances, loses all independence and singleness of character, and degenerates so rapidly from the primitive dignity of his sylvan origin, that it is scarcely possible to indulge in any other expectation, than that the whole species must at length be exterminated by its own infinite imbecility and vileness."

"Your opinions," said Mr Jenkison, a round-faced little gentleman of about forty-five, "seem to differ toto coelo. I have often debated the matter in my own mind, pro and con, and have at length arrived at this conclusion, that there is not in the human race a tendency either to moral perfectibility or deterioration; but that the quantities of each are so exactly balanced by their reciprocal results, that the species, with respect to the sum of good and evil, knowledge and ignorance, happiness and misery, remains exactly and perpetually in statu quo."

"Surely," said Mr Foster, "you cannot maintain such a proposition in the face of evidence so luminous. Look at the progress of all the arts and sciences, see chemistry, botany, astronomy -"

"Surely," said Mr Escot, "experience deposes against you. Look at the rapid growth of corruption, luxury, selfishness -"

"Really, gentlemen," said the Reverend Doctor Gaster, after clearing the husk in his throat with two or three hems, "this is a very sceptical, and, I must say, atheistical conversation, and I should have thought, out of respect to my cloth -"

Here the coach stopped, and the coachman, opening the door, vociferated, "Breakfast, gentlemen;" a sound which so gladdened the ears of the divine, that the alacrity with which he sprang from the vehicle superinduced a distortion of his ankle, and he was obliged to limp into the inn between Mr Escot and Mr Jenkison; the former observing, that he ought to look for nothing but evil, and, therefore, should not be surprised at this little accident; the latter remarking, that the comfort of a good breakfast, and the pain of a sprained ankle, pretty exactly balanced each other.

Chapter II

The Squire - The Breakfast

Squire Headlong, in the meanwhile, was quadripartite in his locality; that is to say, he was superintending the operations in four scenes of action, namely, the cellar, the library, the picture-gallery, and the dining-room, preparing for the reception of his philosophical and dilettanti visitors. His myrmidon on this occasion was a little red-nosed butler, whom nature seemed to have cast in the genuine mould of an antique Silenus, and who waddled about the house after his master, wiping his forehead and panting for breath, while the latter bounced from room to room like a cracker, and was indefatigable in his requisitions for the proximity of his vinous Achates, whose advice and co-operation he deemed no less necessary in the library than in the cellar. Multitudes of packages had arrived, by land and water, from London, and Liverpool, and Chester, and Manchester, and Birmingham, and various parts of the mountains: books, wine, cheese, globes, mathematical instruments, turkeys, telescopes, hams, tongues, microscopes, quadrants, sextants, fiddles, flutes, tea, sugar, electrical machines, figs, spices, air-pumps, soda-water, chemical apparatus, eggs, French-horns, drawing books, palettes, oils and colours, bottled ale and porter, scenery for a private theatre, pickles and fish-sauce, patent lamps and chandeliers, barrels of oysters, sofas, chairs, tables, carpets, beds, looking-glasses, pictures, fruits and confections, nuts, oranges, lemons, packages of salt salmon, and jars of Portugal grapes. These, arriving with infinite rapidity, and in inexhaustible succession, had been deposited at random, as the convenience of the moment dictated, sofas in the cellar, chandeliers in the kitchen, hampers of ale in the drawing-room, and fiddles and fish-sauce in the library. The servants, unpacking all these in furious haste, and flying with them from place to place, according to the tumultuous directions of Squire Headlong and the little fat butler who fumed at his heels, chafed, and crossed, and clashed, and tumbled over one another up stairs and down. All was bustle, uproar, and confusion; yet nothing seemed to advance: while the rage and impetuosity of the Squire continued fermenting to the highest degree of exasperation, which he signified, from time to time, by converting some newly unpacked article, such as a book, a bottle, a ham, or a fiddle, into a missile against the head of some unfortunate servant who did not seem to move in a ratio of velocity corresponding to the intensity of his master's desires.

In this state of eager preparation we shall leave the happy inhabitants of Headlong Hall, and return to the three philosophers and the unfortunate divine, whom we left limping with a sprained ankle, into the breakfast-room of the inn; where his two supporters deposited him safely in a large arm-chair, with his wounded leg comfortably stretched out on another. The morning being extremely cold, he contrived to be seated as near the fire as was consistent with his other object of having a perfect command of the table and its apparatus; which consisted not only of the ordinary comforts of tea and toast, but of a delicious supply of new-laid eggs, and a magnificent round of beef; against which Mr Escot immediately pointed all the artillery of his eloquence, declaring the use of animal food, conjointly with that of fire, to be one of the principal causes of the present degeneracy of mankind. "The natural and original man," said he, "lived in the woods: the roots and fruits of the earth supplied his simple nutriment: he had few desires, and no diseases. But, when he began to sacrifice victims on the altar of superstition, to pursue the goat and the deer, and, by the pernicious invention of fire, to pervert their flesh into food, luxury, disease, and premature death, were let loose upon the world. Such is clearly the correct interpretation of the fable of Prometheus, which is the symbolical portraiture of that disastrous epoch, when man first applied fire to culinary purposes, and thereby surrendered his liver to the vulture of disease. From that period the stature of mankind has been in a state of gradual diminution, and I have not the least doubt that it will continue to grow small by degrees, and lamentably less, till the whole race will vanish imperceptibly from the face of the earth."

"I cannot agree," said Mr Foster, "in the consequences being so very disastrous. I admit, that in some respects the use of animal food retards, though it cannot materially inhibit, the perfectibility of the species. But the use of fire was indispensably necessary, as AEschylus and Virgil expressly assert, to give being to the various arts of life, which, in their rapid and interminable progress, will finally conduct every individual of the race to the philosophic pinnacle of pure and perfect felicity."

"In the controversy concerning animal and vegetable food," said Mr Jenkison, "there is much to be said on both sides; and, the question being in equipoise, I content myself with a mixed diet, and make a point of eating whatever is placed before me, provided it be good in its kind."

In this opinion his two brother philosophers practically coincided, though they both ran down the theory as highly detrimental to the best interests of man.

"I am really astonished," said the Reverend Doctor Gaster, gracefully picking off the supernal fragments of an egg he had just cracked, and clearing away a space at the top for the reception of a small piece of butter, "I am really astonished, gentlemen, at the very heterodox opinions I have heard you deliver: since nothing can be more obvious than that all animals were created solely and exclusively for the use of man."

"Even the tiger that devours him?" said Mr Escot.

"Certainly," said Doctor Gaster.

"How do you prove it?" said Mr Escot.

"It requires no proof," said Doctor Gaster: "it is a point of doctrine. It is written, therefore it is so."

"Nothing can be more logical," said Mr Jenkison. "It has been said," continued he, "that the ox was expressly made to be eaten by man: it may be said, by a parity of reasoning, that man was expressly made to be eaten by the tiger: but as wild oxen exist where there are no men, and men where there are no tigers, it would seem that in these instances they do not properly answer the ends of their creation."

"It is a mystery," said Doctor Gaster.

"Not to launch into the question of final causes," said Mr Escot, helping himself at the same time to a slice of beef, "concerning which I will candidly acknowledge I am as profoundly ignorant as the most dogmatical theologian possibly can be, I just wish to observe, that the pure and peaceful manners which Homer ascribes to the Lotophagi, and which at this day characterise many nations (the Hindoos, for example, who subsist exclusively on the fruits of the earth), depose very strongly in favour of a vegetable regimen."

"It may be said, on the contrary," said Mr Foster, "that animal food acts on the mind as manure does on flowers, forcing them into a degree of expansion they would not otherwise have attained. If we can imagine a philosophical auricula falling into a train of theoretical meditation on its original and natural nutriment, till it should work itself up into a profound abomination of bullock's blood, sugar-baker's scum, and other unnatural ingredients of that rich composition of soil which had brought it to perfection[2.1], and insist on being planted in common earth, it would have all the advantage of natural theory on its side that the most strenuous advocate of the vegetable system could desire; but it would soon discover the practical error of its retrograde experiment by its lamentable inferiority in strength and beauty to all the auriculas around it. I am afraid, in some instances at least, this analogy holds true with respect to mind. No one will make a comparison, in point of mental power, between the Hindoos and the ancient Greeks."

"The anatomy of the human stomach," said Mr Escot, "and the formation of the teeth, clearly place man in the class of frugivorous animals."

"Many anatomists," said Mr Foster, "are of a different opinion, and agree in discerning the characteristics of the carnivorous classes."

"I am no anatomist," said Mr Jenkison, "and cannot decide where doctors disagree; in the meantime, I conclude that man is omnivorous, and on that conclusion I act."

"Your conclusion is truly orthodox," said the Reverend Doctor Gaster: "indeed, the loaves and fishes are typical of a mixed diet; and the practice of the Church in all ages shows -"

"That it never loses sight of the loaves and fishes," said Mr Escot.

"It never loses sight of any point of sound doctrine," said the reverend doctor.

The coachman now informed them their time was elapsed; nor could all the pathetic remonstrances of the reverend divine, who declared he had not half breakfasted, succeed in gaining one minute from the inexorable Jehu.

"You will allow," said Mr Foster, as soon as they were again in motion, "that the wild man of the woods could not transport himself over two hundred miles of forest, with as much facility as one of these vehicles transports you and me through the heart of this cultivated country."

"I am certain," said Mr Escot, "that a wild man can travel an immense distance without fatigue; but what is the advantage of locomotion? The wild man is happy in one spot, and there he remains: the civilised man is wretched in every place he happens to be in, and then congratulates himself on being accommodated with a machine, that will whirl him to another, where he will be just as miserable as ever."

We shall now leave the mail-coach to find its way to Capel Cerig, the nearest point of the Holyhead road to the dwelling of Squire Headlong.

Chapter III

The Arrivals

In the midst of that scene of confusion thrice confounded, in which we left the inhabitants of Headlong Hall, arrived the lovely Caprioletta Headlong, the Squire's sister (whom he had sent for, from the residence of her maiden aunt at Caernarvon, to do the honours of his house), beaming like light on chaos, to arrange disorder and harmonise discord. The tempestuous spirit of her brother became instantaneously as smooth as the surface of the lake of Llanberris; and the little fat butler "plessed Cot, and St Tafit, and the peautiful tamsel," for being permitted to move about the house in his natural pace. In less than twenty-four hours after her arrival, everything was disposed in its proper station, and the Squire began to be all impatience for the appearance of his promised guests.

The first visitor with whom he had the felicity of shaking hands was Marmaduke Milestone, Esquire, who arrived with a portfolio under his arm. Mr Milestone[3.1] was a picturesque landscape gardener of the first celebrity, who was not without hopes of persuading Squire Headlong to put his romantic pleasure-grounds under a process of improvement, promising himself a signal triumph for his incomparable art in the difficult and, therefore, glorious achievement of polishing and trimming the rocks of Llanberris.

Next arrived a post-chaise from the inn at Capel Cerig, containing the Reverend Doctor Gaster. It appeared, that, when the mail-coach deposited its valuable cargo, early on the second morning, at the inn at Capel Cerig, there was only one post-chaise to be had; it was therefore determined that the reverend Doctor and the luggage should proceed in the chaise, and that the three philosophers should walk. When the reverend gentleman first seated himself in the chaise, the windows were down all round; but he allowed it to drive off under the idea that he could easily pull them up. This task, however, he had considerable difficulty in accomplishing, and when he had succeeded, it availed him little; for the frames and glasses had long since discontinued their ancient familiarity. He had, however, no alternative but to proceed, and to comfort himself, as he went, with some choice quotations from the book of Job. The road led along the edges of tremendous chasms, with torrents dashing in the bottom; so that, if his teeth had not chattered with cold, they would have done so with fear. The Squire shook him heartily by the hand, and congratulated him on his safe arrival at Headlong Hall. The Doctor returned the squeeze, and assured him that the congratulation was by no means misapplied.

Next came the three philosophers, highly delighted with their walk, and full of rapturous exclamations on the sublime beauties of the scenery.

The Doctor shrugged up his shoulders, and confessed he preferred the scenery of Putney and Kew, where a man could go comfortably to sleep in his chaise, without being in momentary terror of being hurled headlong down a precipice.

Mr Milestone observed, that there were great capabilities in the scenery, but it wanted shaving and polishing. If he could but have it under his care for a single twelvemonth, he assured them no one would be able to know it again.

Mr Jenkison thought the scenery was just what it ought to be, and required no alteration.

Mr Foster thought it could be improved, but doubted if that effect would be produced by the system of Mr Milestone.

Mr Escot did not think that any human being could improve it, but had no doubt of its having changed very considerably for the worse, since the days when the now barren rocks were covered with the immense forest of Snowdon, which must have contained a very fine race of wild men, not less than ten feet high.

The next arrival was that of Mr Cranium, and his lovely daughter Miss Cephalis Cranium, who flew to the arms of her dear friend Caprioletta, with all that warmth of friendship which young ladies usually assume towards each other in the presence of young gentlemen.[3.2]

Miss Cephalis blushed like a carnation at the sight of Mr Escot, and Mr Escot glowed like a corn-poppy at the sight of Miss Cephalis. It was at least obvious to all observers, that he could imagine the possibility of one change for the better, even in this terrestrial theatre of universal deterioration.

Mr Cranium's eyes wandered from Mr Escot to his daughter, and from his daughter to Mr Escot; and his complexion, in the course of the scrutiny, underwent several variations, from the dark red of the peony to the deep blue of the convolvulus.

Mr Escot had formerly been the received lover of Miss Cephalis, till he incurred the indignation of her father by laughing at a very profound craniological dissertation which the old gentleman delivered; nor had Mr Escot yet discovered the means of mollifying his wrath.

Mr Cranium carried in his own hands a bag, the contents of which were too precious to be intrusted to any one but himself; and earnestly entreated to be shown to the chamber appropriated for his reception, that he might deposit his treasure in safety. The little butler was accordingly summoned to conduct him to his cubiculum.

Next arrived a post-chaise, carrying four insides, whose extreme thinness enabled them to travel thus economically without experiencing the slightest inconvenience. These four personages were, two very profound critics, Mr Gall and Mr Treacle, who followed the trade of reviewers, but occasionally indulged themselves in the composition of bad poetry; and two very multitudinous versifiers, Mr Nightshade and Mr Mac Laurel, who followed the trade of poetry, but occasionally indulged themselves in the composition of bad criticism. Mr Nightshade and Mr Mac Laurel were the two senior lieutenants of a very formidable corps of critics, of whom Timothy Treacle, Esquire, was captain, and Geoffrey Gall, Esquire, generalissimo.

The last arrivals were Mr Cornelius Chromatic, the most profound and scientific of all amateurs of the fiddle, with his two blooming daughters, Miss Tenorina and Miss Graziosa; Sir Patrick O'Prism, a dilettante painter of high renown, and his maiden aunt, Miss Philomela Poppyseed, an indefatigable compounder of novels, written for the express purpose of supporting every species of superstition and prejudice; and Mr Panscope, the chemical, botanical, geological, astronomical, mathematical, metaphysical, meteorological, anatomical, physiological, galvanistical, musical, pictorial, bibliographical, critical philosopher, who had run through the whole circle of the sciences, and understood them all equally well.

Mr Milestone was impatient to take a walk round the grounds, that he might examine how far the system of clumping and levelling could be carried advantageously into effect. The ladies retired to enjoy each other's society in the first happy moments of meeting: the Reverend Doctor Gaster sat by the library fire, in profound meditation over a volume of the "Almanach des Gourmands:" Mr Panscope sat in the opposite corner with a volume of Rees' Cyclopaedia: Mr Cranium was busy upstairs: Mr Chromatic retreated to the music-room, where he fiddled through a book of solos before the ringing of the first dinner bell. The remainder of the party supported Mr Milestone's proposition; and, accordingly, Squire Headlong and Mr Milestone leading the van, they commenced their perambulation.

Chapter IV

The Grounds

"I perceive," said Mr Milestone, after they had walked a few paces, "these grounds have never been touched by the finger of taste."

"The place is quite a wilderness," said Squire Headlong: "for, during the latter part of my father's life, while I was finishing my education, he troubled himself about nothing but the cellar, and suffered everything else to go to rack and ruin. A mere wilderness, as you see, even now in December; but in summer a complete nursery of briers, a forest of thistles, a plantation of nettles, without any live stock but goats, that have eaten up all the bark of the trees. Here you see is the pedestal of a statue, with only half a leg and four toes remaining: there were many here once. When I was a boy, I used to sit every day on the shoulders of Hercules: what became of him I have never been able to ascertain. Neptune has been lying these seven years in the dust-hole; Atlas had his head knocked off to fit him for propping a shed; and only the day before yesterday we fished Bacchus out of the horse-pond."

"My dear sir," said Mr Milestone, "accord me your permission to wave the wand of enchantment over your grounds. The rocks shall be blown up, the trees shall be cut down, the wilderness and all its goats shall vanish like mist. Pagodas and Chinese bridges, gravel walks and shrubberies, bowling-greens, canals, and clumps of larch, shall rise upon its ruins. One age, sir, has brought to light the treasures of ancient learning; a second has penetrated into the depths of metaphysics; a third has brought to perfection the science of astronomy; but it was reserved for the exclusive genius of the present times, to invent the noble art of picturesque gardening, which has given, as it were, a new tint to the complexion of nature, and a new outline to the physiognomy of the universe!"

"Give me leave," said Sir Patrick O'Prism, "to take an exception to that same. Your system of levelling, and trimming, and clipping, and docking, and clumping, and polishing, and cropping, and shaving, destroys all the beautiful intricacies of natural luxuriance, and all the graduated harmonies of light and shade, melting into one another, as you see them on that rock over yonder. I never saw one of your improved places, as you call them, and which are nothing but big bowling-greens, like sheets of green paper, with a parcel of round clumps scattered over them, like so many spots of ink, flicked at random out of a pen,[4.1] and a solitary animal here and there looking as if it were lost, that I did not think it was for all the world like Hounslow Heath, thinly sprinkled over with bushes and highwaymen."

"Sir," said Mr Milestone, "you will have the goodness to make a distinction between the picturesque and the beautiful."

"Will I?" said Sir Patrick, "och! but I won't. For what is beautiful? That what pleases the eye. And what pleases the eye? Tints variously broken and blended. Now, tints variously broken and blended constitute the picturesque."

"Allow me," said Mr Gall. "I distinguish the picturesque and the beautiful, and I add to them, in the laying out of grounds, a third and distinct character, which I call unexpectedness."

"Pray, sir," said Mr Milestone, "by what name do you distinguish this character, when a person walks round the grounds for the second time?"[4.2]

Mr Gall bit his lips, and inwardly vowed to revenge himself on Milestone, by cutting up his next publication.

A long controversy now ensued concerning the picturesque and the beautiful, highly edifying to Squire Headlong.

The three philosophers stopped, as they wound round a projecting point of rock, to contemplate a little boat which was gliding over the tranquil surface of the lake below.

"The blessings of civilisation," said Mr Foster, "extend themselves to the meanest individuals of the community. That boatman, singing as he sails along, is, I have no doubt, a very happy, and, comparatively to the men of his class some centuries back, a very enlightened and intelligent man."

"As a partisan of the system of the moral perfectibility of the human race," said Mr Escot, who was always for considering things on a large scale, and whose thoughts immediately wandered from the lake to the ocean, from the little boat to a ship of the line, "you will probably be able to point out to me the degree of improvement that you suppose to have taken place in the character of a sailor, from the days when Jason sailed through the Cyanean Symplegades, or Noah moored his ark on the summit of Ararat."

"If you talk to me," said Mr Foster, "of mythological personages, of course I cannot meet you on fair grounds."

"We will begin, if you please, then," said Mr Escot, "no further back than the battle of Salamis; and I will ask you if you think the mariners of England are, in any one respect, morally or intellectually, superior to those who then preserved the liberties of Greece, under the direction of Themistocles?"

"I will venture to assert," said Mr Foster, "that considered merely as sailors, which is the only fair mode of judging them, they are as far superior to the Athenians, as the structure of our ships is superior to that of theirs. Would not one English seventy-four, think you, have been sufficient to have sunk, burned, and put to flight, all the Persian and Grecian vessels in that memorable bay? Contemplate the progress of naval architecture, and the slow, but immense succession of concatenated intelligence, by which it has gradually attained its present stage of perfectibility. In this, as in all other branches of art and science, every generation possesses all the knowledge of the preceding, and adds to it its own discoveries in a progression to which there seems no limit. The skill requisite to direct these immense machines is proportionate to their magnitude and complicated mechanism; and, therefore, the English sailor, considered merely as a sailor, is vastly superior to the ancient Greek."

"You make a distinction, of course," said Mr Escot, "between scientific and moral perfectibility?"

"I conceive," said Mr Foster, "that men are virtuous in proportion as they are enlightened; and that, as every generation increases in knowledge, it also increases in virtue."

"I wish it were so," said Mr Escot; "but to me the very reverse appears to be the fact. The progress of knowledge is not general: it is confined to a chosen few of every age. How far these are better than their neighbours, we may examine by and bye. The mass of mankind is composed of beasts of burden, mere clods, and tools of their superiors. By enlarging and complicating your machines, you degrade, not exalt, the human animals you employ to direct them. When the boatswain of a seventy-four pipes all hands to the main tack, and flourishes his rope's end over the shoulders of the poor fellows who are tugging at the ropes, do you perceive so dignified, so gratifying a picture, as Ulysses exhorting his dear friends, his ERIAERES 'ETAIROI, to ply their oars with energy? You will say, Ulysses was a fabulous character. But the economy of his vessel is drawn from nature. Every man on board has a character and a will of his own. He talks to them, argues with them, convinces them; and they obey him, because they love him, and know the reason of his orders. Now, as I have said before, all singleness of character is lost. We divide men into herds like cattle: an individual man, if you strip him of all that is extraneous to himself, is the most wretched and contemptible creature on the face of the earth. The sciences advance. True. A few years of study puts a modern mathematician in possession of more than Newton knew, and leaves him at leisure to add new discoveries of his own. Agreed. But does this make him a Newton? Does it put him in possession of that range of intellect, that grasp of mind, from which the discoveries of Newton sprang? It is mental power that I look for: if you can demonstrate the increase of that, I will give up the field. Energy, independence, individuality, disinterested virtue, active benevolence, self-oblivion, universal philanthropy, these are the qualities I desire to find, and of which I contend that every succeeding age produces fewer examples. I repeat it; there is scarcely such a thing to be found as a single individual man; a few classes compose the whole frame of society, and when you know one of a class you know the whole of it. Give me the wild man of the woods; the original, unthinking, unscientific, unlogical savage: in him there is at least some good; but, in a civilised, sophisticated, cold-blooded, mechanical, calculating slave of Mammon and the world, there is none, absolutely none. Sir, if I fall into a river, an unsophisticated man will jump in and bring me out; but a philosopher will look on with the utmost calmness, and consider me in the light of a projectile, and, making a calculation of the degree of force with which I have impinged the surface, the resistance of the fluid, the velocity of the current, and the depth of the water in that particular place, he will ascertain with the greatest nicety in what part of the mud at the bottom I may probably be found, at any given distance of time from the moment of my first immersion."

Mr Foster was preparing to reply, when the first dinner-bell rang, and he immediately commenced a precipitate return towards the house; followed by his two companions, who both admitted that he was now leading the way to at least a temporary period of physical amelioration: "but, alas!" added Mr Escot, after a moment's reflection, "Epulae NOCUERE repostae![4.3]"

Chapter V

The Dinner

The sun was now terminating his diurnal course, and the lights were glittering on the festal board. When the ladies had retired, and the Burgundy had taken two or three tours of the table, the following conversation took place:

Squire Headlong. Push about the bottle: Mr Escot, it stands with you. No heeltaps. As to skylight, liberty-hall.

Mr Mac Laurel. Really, Squire Headlong, this is the vara nectar itsel. Ye hae saretainly discovered the tarrestrial paradise, but it flows wi' a better leecor than milk an' honey.

The Reverend Doctor Gaster. Hem! Mr Mac Laurel! there is a degree of profaneness in that observation, which I should not have looked for in so staunch a supporter of church and state. Milk and honey was the pure food of the antediluvian patriarchs, who knew not the use of the grape, happily for them. (Tossing off a bumper of Burgundy.)

Mr Escot. Happy, indeed! The first inhabitants of the world knew not the use either of wine or animal food; it is, therefore, by no means incredible that they lived to the age of several centuries, free from war, and commerce, and arbitrary government, and every other species of desolating wickedness. But man was then a very different animal to what he now is: he had not the faculty of speech; he was not encumbered with clothes; he lived in the open air; his first step out of which, as Hamlet truly observes, is into his grave[5.1]. His first dwellings, of course, were the hollows of trees and rocks. In process of time he began to build: thence grew villages; thence grew cities. Luxury, oppression, poverty, misery, and disease kept pace with the progress of his pretended improvements, till, from a free, strong, healthy, peaceful animal, he has become a weak, distempered, cruel, carnivorous slave.

The Reverend Doctor Gaster. Your doctrine is orthodox, in so far as you assert that the original man was not encumbered with clothes, and that he lived in the open air; but, as to the faculty of speech, that, it is certain, he had, for the authority of Moses -

Mr Escot. Of course, sir, I do not presume to dissent from the very exalted authority of that most enlightened astronomer and profound cosmogonist, who had, moreover, the advantage of being inspired; but when I indulge myself with a ramble in the fields of speculation, and attempt to deduce what is probable and rational from the sources of analysis, experience, and comparison, I confess I am too often apt to lose sight of the doctrines of that great fountain of theological and geological philosophy.

Squire Headlong. Push about the bottle.

Mr Foster. Do you suppose the mere animal life of a wild man, living on acorns, and sleeping on the ground, comparable in felicity to that of a Newton, ranging through unlimited space, and penetrating into the arcana of universal motion, to that of a Locke, unravelling the labyrinth of mind, to that of a Lavoisier, detecting the minutest combinations of matter, and reducing all nature to its elements, to that of a Shakespeare, piercing and developing the springs of passion, or of a Milton, identifying himself, as it were, with the beings of an invisible world?

Mr Escot. You suppose extreme cases: but, on the score of happiness, what comparison can you make between the tranquil being of the wild man of the woods and the wretched and turbulent existence of Milton, the victim of persecution, poverty, blindness, and neglect? The records of literature demonstrate that Happiness and Intelligence are seldom sisters. Even if it were otherwise, it would prove nothing. The many are always sacrificed to the few. Where one man advances, hundreds retrograde; and the balance is always in favour of universal deterioration.

Mr Foster. Virtue is independent of external circumstances. The exalted understanding looks into the truth of things, and, in its own peaceful contemplations, rises superior to the world. No philosopher would resign his mental acquisitions for the purchase of any terrestrial good.

Mr Escot. In other words, no man whatever would resign his identity, which is nothing more than the consciousness of his perceptions, as the price of any acquisition. But every man, without exception, would willingly effect a very material change in his relative situation to other individuals. Unluckily for the rest of your argument, the understanding of literary people is for the most part exalted, as you express it, not so much by the love of truth and virtue, as by arrogance and self-sufficiency; and there is, perhaps, less disinterestedness, less liberality, less general benevolence, and more envy, hatred, and uncharitableness among them, than among any other description of men.

(The eye of Mr Escot, as he pronounced these words, rested very innocently and unintentionally on Mr Gall.)

Mr Gall. You allude, sir, I presume, to my review.

Mr Escot. Pardon me, sir. You will be convinced it is impossible I can allude to your review, when I assure you that I have never read a single page of it.

Mr Gall, Mr Treacle, Mr Nightshade, and Mr Mac Laurel. Never read our review! ! ! !

Mr Escot. Never. I look on periodical criticism in general to be a species of shop, where panegyric and defamation are sold, wholesale, retail, and for exportation. I am not inclined to be a purchaser of these commodities, or to encourage a trade which I consider pregnant with mischief.

Mr Mac Laurel. I can readily conceive, sir, ye wou'd na wullingly encoorage ony dealer in panegeeric: but, frae the manner in which ye speak o' the first creetics an' scholars o' the age, I shou'd think ye wou'd hae a leetle mair predilaction for deefamation.

Mr Escot. I have no predilection, sir, for defamation. I make a point of speaking the truth on all occasions; and it seldom happens that the truth can be spoken without some stricken deer pronouncing it a libel.

Mr Nightshade. You are perhaps, sir, an enemy to literature in general?

Mr Escot. If I were, sir, I should be a better friend to periodical critics.

Squire Headlong. Buz!

Mr Treacle. May I simply take the liberty to inquire into the basis of your objection?

Mr Escot. I conceive that periodical criticism disseminates superficial knowledge, and its perpetual adjunct, vanity; that it checks in the youthful mind the habit of thinking for itself; that it delivers partial opinions, and thereby misleads the judgment; that it is never conducted with a view to the general interests of literature, but to serve the interested ends of individuals, and the miserable purposes of party.

Mr Mac Laurel. Ye ken, sir, a mon mun leeve.

Mr Escot. While he can live honourably, naturally, justly, certainly: no longer.

Mr Mac Laurel. Every mon, sir, leeves according to his ain notions of honour an' justice: there is a wee defference amang the learned wi' respact to the defineetion o' the terms.

Mr Escot. I believe it is generally admitted that one of the ingredients of justice is disinterestedness.

Mr Mac Laurel. It is na admetted, sir, amang the pheelosophers of Edinbroo', that there is ony sic thing as desenterestedness in the warld, or that a mon can care for onything sae much as his ain sel: for ye mun observe, sir, every mon has his ain parteecular feelings of what is gude, an' beautifu', an' consentaneous to his ain indiveedual nature, an' desires to see every thing aboot him in that parteecular state which is maist conformable to his ain notions o' the moral an' poleetical fetness o' things. Twa men, sir, shall purchase a piece o' grund atween 'em, and ae mon shall cover his half wi' a park -

Mr Milestone. Beautifully laid out in lawns and clumps, with a belt of trees at the circumference, and an artificial lake in the centre.

Mr Mac Laurel. Exactly, sir: an' shall keep it a' for his ain sel: an' the other mon shall divide his half into leetle farms of twa or three acres -

Mr Escot. Like those of the Roman republic, and build a cottage on each of them, and cover his land with a simple, innocent, and smiling population, who shall owe, not only their happiness, but their existence, to his benevolence.

Mr Mac Laurel. Exactly, sir: an' ye will ca' the first mon selfish, an' the second desenterested; but the pheelosophical truth is semply this, that the ane is pleased wi' looking at trees, an' the other wi' seeing people happy an' comfortable. It is aunly a matter of indiveedual feeling. A paisant saves a mon's life for the same reason that a hero or a footpad cuts his thrapple: an' a pheelosopher delevers a mon frae a preson, for the same reason that a tailor or a prime meenester puts him into it: because it is conformable to his ain parteecular feelings o' the moral an' poleetical fetness o' things.

Squire Headlong. Wake the Reverend Doctor. Doctor, the bottle stands with you.

The Reverend Doctor Gaster. It is an error of which I am seldom guilty.

Mr Mac Laurel. Noo, ye ken, sir, every mon is the centre of his ain system, an' endaivours as much as possible to adapt everything aroond him to his ain parteecular views.

Mr Escot. Thus, sir, I presume, it suits the particular views of a poet, at one time to take the part of the people against their oppressors, and at another, to take the part of the oppressors, against the people.

Mr Mac Laurel. Ye mun alloo, sir, that poetry is a sort of ware or commodity, that is brought into the public market wi' a' other descreptions of merchandise, an' that a mon is pairfectly justified in getting the best price he can for his article. Noo, there are three reasons for taking the part o' the people; the first is, when general leeberty an' public happiness are conformable to your ain parteecular feelings o' the moral an' poleetical fetness o' things: the second is, when they happen to be, as it were, in a state of exceetabeelity, an' ye think ye can get a gude price for your commodity, by flingin' in a leetle seasoning o' pheelanthropy an' republican speerit; the third is, when ye think ye can bully the menestry into gieing ye a place or a pansion to hau'd your din, an' in that case, ye point an attack against them within the pale o' the law; an' if they tak nae heed o' ye, ye open a stronger fire; an' the less heed they tak, the mair ye bawl; an' the mair factious ye grow, always within the pale o' the law, till they send a plenipotentiary to treat wi' ye for yoursel, an' then the mair popular ye happen to be, the better price ye fetch.

Squire Headlong. Off with your heeltaps.

Mr Cranium. I perfectly agree with Mr Mac Laurel in his definition of self-love and disinterestedness: every man's actions are determined by his peculiar views, and those views are determined by the organisation of his skull. A man in whom the organ of benevolence is not developed, cannot be benevolent: he in whom it is so, cannot be otherwise. The organ of self-love is prodigiously developed in the greater number of subjects that have fallen under my observation.

Mr Escot. Much less I presume, among savage than civilised men, who, constant only to the love of self, and consistent only in their aim to deceive, are always actuated by the hope of personal advantage, or by the dread of personal punishment[5.2].

Mr Cranium. Very probably.

Mr Escot. You have, of course, found very copious specimens of the organs of hypocrisy, destruction, and avarice.

Mr Cranium. Secretiveness, destructiveness, and covetiveness. You may add, if you please, that of constructiveness.

Mr Escot. Meaning, I presume, the organ of building; which I contend to be not a natural organ of the featherless biped.

Mr Cranium. Pardon me: it is here. (As he said these words, he produced a skull from his pocket, and placed it on the table to the great surprise of the company.) This was the skull of Sir Christopher Wren. You observe this protuberance (The skull was handed round the table.)

Mr Escot. I contend that the original unsophisticated man was by no means constructive. He lived in the open air, under a tree.

The Reverend Doctor Gaster. The tree of life. Unquestionably. Till he had tasted the forbidden fruit.

Mr Jenkison. At which period, probably, the organ of constructiveness was added to his anatomy, as a punishment for his transgression.

Mr Escot. There could not have been a more severe one, since the propensity which has led him to building cities has proved the greatest curse of his existence.

Squire Headlong. (taking the skull.) Memento mori. Come, a bumper of Burgundy.

Mr Nightshade. A very classical application, Squire Headlong. The Romans were in the practice of adhibiting skulls at their banquets, and sometimes little skeletons of silver, as a silent admonition to the guests to enjoy life while it lasted.

The Reverend Doctor Gaster. Sound doctrine, Mr Nightshade.

Mr Escot. I question its soundness. The use of vinous spirit has a tremendous influence in the deterioration of the human race.

Mr Foster. I fear, indeed, it operates as a considerable check to the progress of the species towards moral and intellectual perfection. Yet many great men have been of opinion that it exalts the imagination, fires the genius, accelerates the flow of ideas, and imparts to dispositions naturally cold and deliberative that enthusiastic sublimation which is the source of greatness and energy.

Mr Nightshade. Laudibus arguitur vini vinosus Homerus.[5.3]

Mr Jenkison. I conceive the use of wine to be always pernicious in excess, but often useful in moderation: it certainly kills some, but it saves the lives of others: I find that an occasional glass, taken with judgment and caution, has a very salutary effect in maintaining that equilibrium of the system, which it is always my aim to preserve; and this calm and temperate use of wine was, no doubt, what Homer meant to inculcate, when he said: Par de depas oinoio, piein hote thumos anogoi.[5.4]

Squire Headlong. Good. Pass the bottle. (Un morne silence). Sir Christopher does not seem to have raised our spirits. Chromatic, favour us with a specimen of your vocal powers. Something in point.

Mr Chromatic, without further preface, immediately struck up the following

SONG

In his last binn Sir Peter lies,
Who knew not what it was to frown:
Death took him mellow, by surprise,
And in his cellar stopped him down.
Through all our land we could not boast
A knight more gay, more prompt than he,
To rise and fill a bumper toast,
And pass it round with THREE TIMES THREE.

None better knew the feast to sway,
Or keep Mirth's boat in better trim;
For Nature had but little clay Like that of which she moulded him.
The meanest guest that graced his board
Was there the freest of the free,
His bumper toast when Peter poured,
And passed it round with THREE TIMES THREE.

He kept at true good humour's mark
The social flow of pleasure's tide:
He never made a brow look dark,
Nor caused a tear, but when he died.
No sorrow round his tomb should dwell:
More pleased his gay old ghost would be,
For funeral song, and passing bell,
To hear no sound but THREE TIMES THREE.

(Hammering of knuckles and glasses and shouts of bravo!)

Mr Panscope. (Suddenly emerging from a deep reverie.) I have heard, with the most profound attention, everything which the gentleman on the other side of the table has thought proper to advance on the subject of human deterioration; and I must take the liberty to remark, that it augurs a very considerable degree of presumption in any individual, to set himself up against the authority of so many great men, as may be marshalled in metaphysical phalanx under the opposite banners of the controversy; such as Aristotle, Plato, the scholiast on Aristophanes, St Chrysostom, St Jerome, St Athanasius, Orpheus, Pindar, Simonides, Gronovius, Hemsterhusius, Longinus, Sir Isaac Newton, Thomas Paine, Doctor Paley, the King of Prussia, the King of Poland, Cicero, Monsieur Gautier, Hippocrates, Machiavelli, Milton, Colley Cibber, Bojardo, Gregory Nazianzenus, Locke, D'Alembert, Boccaccio, Daniel Defoe, Erasmus, Doctor Smollett, Zimmermann, Solomon, Confucius, Zoroaster, and Thomas-a-Kempis.

Mr Escot. I presume, sir, you are one of those who value an authority more than a reason.

Mr Panscope. The authority, sir, of all these great men, whose works, as well as the whole of the Encyclopaedia Britannica, the entire series of the Monthly Review, the complete set of the Variorum Classics, and the Memoirs of the Academy of Inscriptions, I have read through from beginning to end, deposes, with irrefragable refutation, against your ratiocinative speculations, wherein you seem desirous, by the futile process of analytical dialectics, to subvert the pyramidal structure of synthetically deduced opinions, which have withstood the secular revolutions of physiological disquisition, and which I maintain to be transcendentally self-evident, categorically certain, and syllogistically demonstrable.

Squire Headlong. Bravo! Pass the bottle. The very best speech that ever was made.

Mr Escot. It has only the slight disadvantage of being unintelligible.

Mr Panscope. I am not obliged, sir, as Dr Johnson observed on a similar occasion, to furnish you with an understanding.

Mr Escot. I fear, sir, you would have some difficulty in furnishing me with such an article from your own stock.

Mr Panscope. 'Sdeath, sir, do you question my understanding?

Mr Escot. I only question, sir, where I expect a reply; which, from things that have no existence, I am not visionary enough to anticipate.

Mr Panscope. I beg leave to observe, sir, that my language was perfectly perspicuous, and etymologically correct; and, I conceive, I have demonstrated what I shall now take the liberty to say in plain terms, that all your opinions are extremely absurd.

Mr Escot. I should be sorry, sir, to advance any opinion that you would not think absurd.

Mr Panscope. Death and fury, sir -

Mr Escot. Say no more, sir. That apology is quite sufficient.

Mr Panscope. Apology, sir?

Mr Escot. Even so, sir. You have lost your temper, which I consider equivalent to a confession that you have the worst of the argument.

Mr Panscope. Lightning and devils! sir -

Squire Headlong. No civil war! Temperance, in the name of Bacchus! A glee! a glee! Music has charms to bend the knotted oak. Sir Patrick, you'll join?

Sir Patrick O'Prism. Troth, with all my heart; for, by my soul, I'm bothered completely.

Squire Headlong. Agreed, then; you, and I, and Chromatic. Bumpers! Come, strike up.

Squire Headlong, Mr Chromatic, and Sir Patrick O'Prism, each holding a bumper, immediately vociferated the following

GLEE
A heeltap! a heeltap! I never could bear it! So fill me a bumper, a bumper of claret! Let the bottle pass freely, don't shirk it nor spare it, For a heeltap! a heeltap! I never could bear it!

No skylight! no twilight! while Bacchus rules o'er us: No thinking! no shrinking! all drinking in chorus: Let us moisten our clay, since 'tis thirsty and porous: No thinking! no shrinking! all drinking in chorus!

GRAND CHORUS
By Squire Headlong, Mr Chromatic, Sir Patrick O'Prism, Mr Panscope, Mr Jenkison, Mr Gall, Mr Treacle, Mr Nightshade, Mr Mac Laurel, Mr Cranium, Mr Milestone, and the Reverend Dr Gaster.

A heeltap! a heeltap! I never could bear it! So fill me a bumper, a bumper of claret! Let the bottle pass freely, don't shirk it nor spare it, For a heeltap! a heeltap! I never could bear it!

'OMADOS KAI DOUPOS OROREI'
The little butler now waddled in with a summons from the ladies to tea and coffee. The squire was unwilling to leave his Burgundy. Mr Escot strenuously urged the necessity of immediate adjournment, observing, that the longer they continued drinking the worse they should be. Mr Foster seconded the motion, declaring the transition from the bottle to female society to be an indisputable amelioration of the state of the sensitive man. Mr Jenkison allowed the squire and his two brother philosophers to settle the point between them, concluding that he was just as well in one place as another. The question of adjournment was then put, and carried by a large majority.

Chapter VI

The Evening

Mr Panscope, highly irritated by the cool contempt with which Mr Escot had treated him, sate sipping his coffee and meditating revenge. He was not long in discovering the passion of his antagonist for the beautiful Cephalis, for whom he had himself a species of predilection; and it was also obvious to him, that there was some lurking anger in the mind of her father, unfavourable to the hopes of his rival. The stimulus of revenge, superadded to that of preconceived inclination, determined him, after due deliberation, to cut out Mr Escot in the young lady's favour. The practicability of this design he did not trouble himself to investigate; for the havoc he had made in the hearts of some silly girls, who were extremely vulnerable to flattery, and who, not understanding a word he said, considered him a prodigious clever man, had impressed him with an unhesitating idea of his own irresistibility. He had not only the requisites already specified for fascinating female vanity, he could likewise fiddle with tolerable dexterity, though by no means so quick as Mr Chromatic (for our readers are of course aware that rapidity of execution, not delicacy of expression, constitutes the scientific perfection of modern music), and could warble a fashionable love-ditty with considerable affectation of feeling: besides this, he was always extremely well dressed, and was heir-apparent to an estate of ten thousand a-year. The influence which the latter consideration might have on the minds of the majority of his female acquaintance, whose morals had been formed by the novels of such writers as Miss Philomela Poppyseed, did not once enter into his calculation of his own personal attractions. Relying, therefore, on past success, he determined to appeal to his fortune, and already, in imagination, considered himself sole lord and master of the affections of the beautiful Cephalis.

Mr Escot and Mr Foster were the only two of the party who had entered the library (to which the ladies had retired, and which was interior to the music-room) in a state of perfect sobriety. Mr Escot had placed himself next to the beautiful Cephalis: Mr Cranium had laid aside much of the terror of his frown; the short craniological conversation, which had passed between him and Mr Escot, had softened his heart in his favour; and the copious libations of Burgundy in which he had indulged had smoothed his brow into unusual serenity.

Mr Foster placed himself near the lovely Caprioletta, whose artless and innocent conversation had already made an impression on his susceptible spirit.

The Reverend Doctor Gaster seated himself in the corner of a sofa near Miss Philomela Poppyseed. Miss Philomela detailed to him the plan of a very moral and aristocratical novel she was preparing for the press, and continued holding forth, with her eyes half shut, till a long-drawn nasal tone from the reverend divine compelled her suddenly to open them in all the indignation of surprise. The cessation of the hum of her voice awakened the reverend gentleman, who, lifting up first one eyelid, then the other, articulated, or rather murmured, "Admirably planned, indeed!"

"I have not quite finished, sir," said Miss Philomela, bridling. "Will you have the goodness to inform me where I left off?"

The doctor hummed a while, and at length answered: "I think you had just laid it down as a position, that a thousand a-year is an indispensable ingredient in the passion of love, and that no man, who is not so far gifted by nature, can reasonably presume to feel that passion himself, or be correctly the object of it with a well-educated female."

"That, sir," said Miss Philomela, highly incensed, "is the fundamental principle which I lay down in the first chapter, and which the whole four volumes, of which I detailed to you the outline, are intended to set in a strong practical light."

"Bless me!" said the doctor, "what a nap I must have had!"

Miss Philomela flung away to the side of her dear friends Gall and Treacle, under whose fostering patronage she had been puffed into an extensive reputation, much to the advantage of the young ladies of the age, whom she taught to consider themselves as a sort of commodity, to be put up at public auction, and knocked down to the highest bidder. Mr Nightshade and Mr Mac Laurel joined the trio; and it was secretly resolved, that Miss Philomela should furnish them with a portion of her manuscripts, and that Messieurs Gall & Co. should devote the following morning to cutting and drying a critique on a work calculated to prove so extensively beneficial, that Mr Gall protested he really envied the writer.

While this amiable and enlightened quintetto were busily employed in flattering one another, Mr Cranium retired to complete the preparations he had begun in the morning for a lecture, with which he intended, on some future evening, to favour the company: Sir Patrick O'Prism walked out into the grounds to study the effect of moonlight on the snow-clad mountains: Mr Foster and Mr Escot continued to make love, and Mr Panscope to digest his plan of attack on the heart of Miss Cephalis: Mr Jenkison sate by the fire, reading Much Ado about Nothing: the Reverend Doctor Gaster was still enjoying the benefit of Miss Philomela's opiate, and serenading the company from his solitary corner: Mr Chromatic was reading music, and occasionally humming a note: and Mr Milestone had produced his portfolio for the edification and amusement of Miss Tenorina, Miss Graziosa, and Squire Headlong, to whom he was pointing out the various beauties of his plan for Lord Littlebrain's park.

Mr Milestone. This, you perceive, is the natural state of one part of the grounds. Here is a wood, never yet touched by the finger of taste; thick, intricate, and gloomy. Here is a little stream, dashing from stone to stone, and overshadowed with these untrimmed boughs.

Miss Tenorina. The sweet romantic spot! How beautifully the birds must sing there on a summer evening!

Miss Graziosa. Dear sister! how can you endure the horrid thicket?

Mr Milestone. You are right, Miss Graziosa: your taste is correct, perfectly en regle. Now, here is the same place corrected, trimmed, polished, decorated, adorned. Here sweeps a plantation, in that beautiful regular curve: there winds a gravel walk: here are parts of the old wood, left in these majestic circular clumps, disposed at equal distances with wonderful symmetry: there are some single shrubs scattered in elegant profusion: here a Portugal laurel, there a juniper; here a laurustinus, there a spruce fir; here a larch, there a lilac; here a rhododendron, there an arbutus. The stream, you see, is become a canal: the banks are perfectly smooth and green, sloping to the water's edge: and there is Lord Littlebrain, rowing in an elegant boat.

Squire Headlong. Magical, faith!

Mr Milestone. Here is another part of the grounds in its natural state. Here is a large rock, with the mountain-ash rooted in its fissures, overgrown, as you see, with ivy and moss; and from this part of it bursts a little fountain, that runs bubbling down its rugged sides.

Miss Tenorina. O how beautiful! How I should love the melody of that miniature cascade!

Mr Milestone. Beautiful, Miss Tenorina! Hideous. Base, common, and popular. Such a thing as you may see anywhere, in wild and mountainous districts. Now, observe the metamorphosis. Here is the same rock, cut into the shape of a giant. In one hand he holds a horn, through which that little fountain is thrown to a prodigious elevation. In the other is a ponderous stone, so exactly balanced as to be apparently ready to fall on the head of any person who may happen to be beneath[6.1]: and there is Lord Littlebrain walking under it.

Squire Headlong. Miraculous, by Mahomet!

Mr Milestone. This is the summit of a hill, covered, as you perceive, with wood, and with those mossy stones scattered at random under the trees.

Miss Tenorina. What a delightful spot to read in, on a summer's day! The air must be so pure, and the wind must sound so divinely in the tops of those old pines!

Mr Milestone. Bad taste, Miss Tenorina. Bad taste, I assure you. Here is the spot improved. The trees are cut down: the stones are cleared away: this is an octagonal pavilion, exactly on the centre of the summit: and there you see Lord Littlebrain, on the top of the pavilion, enjoying the prospect with a telescope.

Squire Headlong. Glorious, egad!

Mr Milestone. Here is a rugged mountainous road, leading through impervious shades: the ass and the four goats characterise a wild uncultured scene. Here, as you perceive, it is totally changed into a beautiful gravel-road, gracefully curving through a belt of limes: and there is Lord Littlebrain driving four-in-hand.

Squire Headlong. Egregious, by Jupiter!

Mr Milestone. Here is Littlebrain Castle, a Gothic, moss-grown structure, half bosomed in trees. Near the casement of that turret is an owl peeping from the ivy.

Squire Headlong. And devilish wise he looks.

Mr Milestone. Here is the new house, without a tree near it, standing in the midst of an undulating lawn: a white, polished, angular building, reflected to a nicety in this waveless lake: and there you see Lord Littlebrain looking out of the window.

Squire Headlong. And devilish wise he looks too. You shall cut me a giant before you go.

Mr Milestone. Good. I'll order down my little corps of pioneers.

During this conversation, a hot dispute had arisen between Messieurs Gall and Nightshade; the latter pertinaciously insisting on having his new poem reviewed by Treacle, who he knew would extol it most loftily, and not by Gall, whose sarcastic commendation he held in superlative horror. The remonstrances of Squire Headlong silenced the disputants, but did not mollify the inflexible Gall, nor appease the irritated Nightshade, who secretly resolved that, on his return to London, he would beat his drum in Grub Street, form a mastigophoric corps of his own, and hoist the standard of determined opposition against this critical Napoleon.

Sir Patrick O'Prism now entered, and, after some rapturous exclamations on the effect of the mountain-moonlight, entreated that one of the young ladies would favour him with a song. Miss Tenorina and Miss Graziosa now enchanted the company with some very scientific compositions, which, as usual, excited admiration and astonishment in every one, without a single particle of genuine pleasure. The beautiful Cephalis being then summoned to take her station at the harp, sang with feeling and simplicity the following air:

LOVE AND OPPORTUNITY

Oh! who art thou, so swiftly flying?
My name is Love, the child replied:
Swifter I pass than south-winds sighing,
Or streams, through summer vales that glide.

And who art thou, his flight pursuing? 'Tis cold
Neglect whom now you see:
The little god you there are viewing,
Will die, if once he's touched by me.

Oh! who art thou so fast proceeding,
Ne'er glancing back thine eyes of flame?
Marked but by few, through earth I'm speeding,
And Opportunity's my name.
What form is that, which scowls beside thee?
Repentance is the form you see:
Learn then, the fate may yet betide thee:
She seizes them who seize not me.[6.2]

The little butler now appeared with a summons to supper, shortly after which the party dispersed
for the night.

Chapter VII

The Walk

It was an old custom in Headlong Hall to have breakfast ready at eight, and continue it till two; that
the various guests might rise at their own hour, breakfast when they came down, and employ the
morning as they thought proper; the squire only expecting that they should punctually assemble at
dinner. During the whole of this period, the little butler stood sentinel at a side-table near the fire,
copiously furnished with all the apparatus of tea, coffee, chocolate, milk, cream, eggs, rolls, toast,
muffins, bread, butter, potted beef, cold fowl and partridge, ham, tongue, and anchovy. The
Reverend Doctor Gaster found himself rather queasy in the morning, therefore preferred
breakfasting in bed, on a mug of buttered ale and an anchovy toast. The three philosophers made
their appearance at eight, and enjoyed les premices des depouilles. Mr Foster proposed that, as it
was a fine frosty morning, and they were all good pedestrians, they should take a walk to Tremadoc,
to see the improvements carrying on in that vicinity. This being readily acceded to, they began their
walk.

After their departure, appeared Squire Headlong and Mr Milestone, who agreed, over their muffin
and partridge, to walk together to a ruined tower, within the precincts of the squire's grounds, which
Mr Milestone thought he could improve.

The other guests dropped in by ones and twos, and made their respective arrangements for the
morning. Mr Panscope took a little ramble with Mr Cranium, in the course of which, the former
professed a great enthusiasm for the science of craniology, and a great deal of love for the beautiful
Cephalis, adding a few words about his expectations; the old gentleman was unable to withstand
this triple battery, and it was accordingly determined, after the manner of the heroic age, in which it
was deemed superfluous to consult the opinions and feelings of the lady, as to the manner in which
she should be disposed of, that the lovely Miss Cranium should be made the happy bride of the
accomplished Mr Panscope. We shall leave them for the present to settle preliminaries, while we
accompany the three philosophers in their walk to Tremadoc.

The vale contracted as they advanced, and, when they had passed the termination of the lake, their road wound along a narrow and romantic pass, through the middle of which an impetuous torrent dashed over vast fragments of stone. The pass was bordered on both sides by perpendicular rocks, broken into the wildest forms of fantastic magnificence.

"These are, indeed," said Mr Escot, "confracti mundi rudera[7.1]: yet they must be feeble images of the valleys of the Andes, where the philosophic eye may contemplate, in their utmost extent, the effects of that tremendous convulsion which destroyed the perpendicularity of the poles, and inundated this globe with that torrent of physical evil, from which the greater torrent of moral evil has issued, that will continue to roll on, with an expansive power and an accelerated impetus, till the whole human race shall be swept away in its vortex."

"The precession of the equinoxes," said Mr Foster, "will gradually ameliorate the physical state of our planet, till the ecliptic shall again coincide with the equator, and the equal diffusion of light and heat over the whole surface of the earth typify the equal and happy existence of man, who will then have attained the final step of pure and perfect intelligence."

"It is by no means clear," said Mr Jenkison, "that the axis of the earth was ever perpendicular to the plane of its orbit, or that it ever will be so. Explosion and convulsion are necessary to the maintenance of either hypothesis: for La Place has demonstrated, that the precession of the equinoxes is only a secular equation of a very long period, which, of course, proves nothing either on one side or the other."

They now emerged, by a winding ascent, from the vale of Llanberris, and after some little time arrived at Bedd Gelert. Proceeding through the sublimely romantic pass of Aberglaslynn, their road led along the edge of Traeth Mawr, a vast arm of the sea, which they then beheld in all the magnificence of the flowing tide. Another five miles brought them to the embankment, which has since been completed, and which, by connecting the two counties of Meirionnydd and Caernarvon, excludes the sea from an extensive tract. The embankment, which was carried on at the same time from both the opposite coasts, was then very nearly meeting in the centre. They walked to the extremity of that part of it which was thrown out from the Caernarvonshire shore. The tide was now ebbing: it had filled the vast basin within, forming a lake about five miles in length and more than one in breadth. As they looked upwards with their backs to the open sea, they beheld a scene which no other in this country can parallel, and which the admirers of the magnificence of nature will ever remember with regret, whatever consolation may be derived from the probable utility of the works which have excluded the waters from their ancient receptacle. Vast rocks and precipices, intersected with little torrents, formed the barrier on the left: on the right, the triple summit of Moelwyn reared its majestic boundary: in the depth was that sea of mountains, the wild and stormy outline of the Snowdonian chain, with the giant Wyddfa towering in the midst. The mountain-frame remains unchanged, unchangeable: but the liquid mirror it enclosed is gone.

The tide ebbed with rapidity: the waters within, retained by the embankment, poured through its two points an impetuous cataract, curling and boiling in innumerable eddies, and making a tumultuous melody admirably in unison with the surrounding scene. The three philosophers looked on in silence; and at length unwillingly turned away, and proceeded to the little town of Tremadoc, which is built on land recovered in a similar manner from the sea. After inspecting the manufactories, and refreshing themselves at the inn on a cold saddle of mutton and a bottle of sherry, they retraced their steps towards Headlong Hall, commenting as they went on the various objects they had seen.

Mr Escot. I regret that time did not allow us to see the caves on the sea-shore. There is one of which the depth is said to be unknown. There is a tradition in the country, that an adventurous fiddler once resolved to explore it; that he entered, and never returned; but that the subterranean sound of a fiddle was heard at a farm-house seven miles inland. It is, therefore, concluded that he lost his way in the labyrinth of caverns, supposed to exist under the rocky soil of this part of the country.

Mr Jenkison. A supposition that must always remain in force, unless a second fiddler, equally adventurous and more successful, should return with an accurate report of the true state of the fact.

Mr Foster. What think you of the little colony we have just been inspecting; a city, as it were, in its cradle?

Mr Escot. With all the weakness of infancy, and all the vices of maturer age. I confess, the sight of those manufactories, which have suddenly sprung up, like fungous excrescences, in the bosom of these wild and desolate scenes, impressed me with as much horror and amazement as the sudden appearance of the stocking manufactory struck into the mind of Rousseau, when, in a lonely valley of the Alps, he had just congratulated himself on finding a spot where man had never been.

Mr Foster. The manufacturing system is not yet purified from some evils which necessarily attend it, but which I conceive are greatly overbalanced by their concomitant advantages. Contemplate the vast sum of human industry to which this system so essentially contributes: seas covered with vessels, ports resounding with life, profound researches, scientific inventions, complicated mechanism, canals carried over deep valleys, and through the bosoms of hills: employment and existence thus given to innumerable families, and the multiplied comforts and conveniences of life diffused over the whole community.

Mr Escot. You present to me a complicated picture of artificial life, and require me to admire it. Seas covered with vessels: every one of which contains two or three tyrants, and from fifty to a thousand slaves, ignorant, gross, perverted, and active only in mischief. Ports resounding with life: in other words, with noise and drunkenness, the mingled din of avarice, intemperance, and prostitution. Profound researches, scientific inventions: to what end? To contract the sum of human wants? to teach the art of living on a little? to disseminate independence, liberty, and health? No; to multiply factitious desires, to stimulate depraved appetites, to invent unnatural wants, to heap up incense on the shrine of luxury, and accumulate expedients of selfish and ruinous profusion. Complicated machinery: behold its blessings. Twenty years ago, at the door of every cottage sate the good woman with her spinning-wheel: the children, if not more profitably employed than in gathering heath and sticks, at least laid in a stock of health and strength to sustain the labours of maturer years. Where is the spinning-wheel now, and every simple and insulated occupation of the industrious cottager? Wherever this boasted machinery is established, the children of the poor are death-doomed from their cradles. Look for one moment at midnight into a cotton-mill, amidst the smell of oil, the smoke of lamps, the rattling of wheels, the dizzy and complicated motions of diabolical mechanism: contemplate the little human machines that keep play with the revolutions of the iron work, robbed at that hour of their natural rest, as of air and exercise by day: observe their pale and ghastly features, more ghastly in that baleful and malignant light, and tell me if you do not fancy yourself on the threshold of Virgil's hell, where

Continuo auditae voces, vagitus et ingens, Infantumque animae flentes, in limine primo, Quos dulcis vitae exsortes, et ab ubere raptos, Abstulit atra dies, et FUNERE MERSIT ACERBO!

As Mr Escot said this, a little rosy-cheeked girl, with a basket of heath on her head, came tripping down the side of one of the rocks on the left. The force of contrast struck even on the phlegmatic spirit of Mr Jenkison, and he almost inclined for a moment to the doctrine of deterioration. Mr Escot continued:

Mr Escot. Nor is the lot of the parents more enviable. Sedentary victims of unhealthy toil, they have neither the corporeal energy of the savage, nor the mental acquisitions of the civilised man. Mind, indeed, they have none, and scarcely animal life. They are mere automata, component parts of the enormous machines which administer to the pampered appetites of the few, who consider themselves the most valuable portion of a state, because they consume in indolence the fruits of the earth, and contribute nothing to the benefit of the community.

Mr Jenkison. That these are evils cannot be denied; but they have their counterbalancing advantages. That a man should pass the day in a furnace and the night in a cellar, is bad for the individual, but good for others who enjoy the benefit of his labour.

Mr Escot. By what right do they so?

Mr Jenkison. By the right of all property and all possession: le droit du plus fort.

Mr Escot. Do you justify that principle?

Mr Jenkison. I neither justify nor condemn it. It is practically recognised in all societies; and, though it is certainly the source of enormous evil, I conceive it is also the source of abundant good, or it would not have so many supporters.

Mr Escot. That is by no means a consequence. Do we not every day see men supporting the most enormous evils, which they know to be so with respect to others, and which in reality are so with respect to themselves, though an erroneous view of their own miserable self-interest induces them to think otherwise?

Mr Jenkison. Good and evil exist only as they are perceived. I cannot therefore understand, how that which a man perceives to be good can be in reality an evil to him: indeed, the word reality only signifies strong belief.

Mr Escot. The views of such a man I contend are false. If he could be made to see the truth -

Mr Jenkison. He sees his own truth. Truth is that which a man troweth. Where there is no man there is no truth. Thus the truth of one is not the truth of another.[7.2]

Mr Foster. I am aware of the etymology; but I contend that there is an universal and immutable truth, deducible from the nature of things.

Mr Jenkison. By whom deducible? Philosophers have investigated the nature of things for centuries, yet no two of them will agree in trowing the same conclusion.

Mr Foster. The progress of philosophical investigation, and the rapidly increasing accuracy of human knowledge, approximate by degrees the diversities of opinion; so that, in process of time, moral science will be susceptible of mathematical demonstration; and, clear and indisputable principles being universally recognised, the coincidence of deduction will necessarily follow.

Mr Escot. Possibly when the inroads of luxury and disease shall have exterminated nine hundred and ninety-nine thousand nine hundred and ninety-nine of every million of the human race, the remaining fractional units may congregate into one point, and come to something like the same conclusion.

Mr Jenkison. I doubt it much. I conceive, if only we three were survivors of the whole system of terrestrial being, we should never agree in our decisions as to the cause of the calamity.

Mr Escot. Be that as it may, I think you must at least assent to the following positions: that the many are sacrificed to the few; that ninety-nine in a hundred are occupied in a perpetual struggle for the preservation of a perilous and precarious existence, while the remaining one wallows in all the redundancies of luxury that can be wrung from their labours and privations; that luxury and liberty are incompatible; and that every new want you invent for civilised man is a new instrument of torture for him who cannot indulge it.

They had now regained the shores of the lake, when the conversation was suddenly interrupted by a tremendous explosion, followed by a violent splashing of water, and various sounds of tumult and confusion, which induced them to quicken their pace towards the spot whence they proceeded.

Chapter VIII

The Tower

In all the thoughts, words, and actions of Squire Headlong, there was a remarkable alacrity of progression, which almost annihilated the interval between conception and execution. He was utterly regardless of obstacles, and seemed to have expunged their very name from his vocabulary. His designs were never nipped in their infancy by the contemplation of those trivial difficulties which often turn awry the current of enterprise; and, though the rapidity of his movements was sometimes arrested by a more formidable barrier, either naturally existing in the pursuit he had undertaken, or created by his own impetuosity, he seldom failed to succeed either in knocking it down or cutting his way through it. He had little idea of gradation: he saw no interval between the first step and the last, but pounced upon his object with the impetus of a mountain cataract. This rapidity of movement, indeed, subjected him to some disasters which cooler spirits would have escaped. He was an excellent sportsman, and almost always killed his game; but now and then he killed his dog.[8.1] Rocks, streams, hedges, gates, and ditches, were objects of no account in his estimation; though a dislocated shoulder, several severe bruises, and two or three narrow escapes for his neck, might have been expected to teach him a certain degree of caution in effecting his transitions. He was so singularly alert in climbing precipices and traversing torrents, that, when he went out on a shooting party, he was very soon left to continue his sport alone, for he was sure to dash up or down some nearly perpendicular path, where no one else had either ability or inclination to follow. He had a pleasure boat on the lake, which he steered with amazing dexterity; but as he always indulged himself in the utmost possible latitude of sail, he was occasionally upset by a sudden gust, and was indebted to his skill in the art of swimming for the opportunity of tempering with a copious libation of wine the unnatural frigidity introduced into his stomach by the extraordinary intrusion of water, an element which he had religiously determined should never pass his lips, but of which, on these occasions, he was sometimes compelled to swallow no inconsiderable quantity. This circumstance alone, of the various disasters that befell him, occasioned him any permanent affliction, and he accordingly noted the day in his pocket-book as a dies nefastus, with this simple abstract, and brief chronicle of the calamity: Mem. Swallowed two or three pints of water: without any notice whatever of the concomitant circumstances. These days, of which there were several, were set apart in Headlong Hall for the purpose of anniversary expiation; and, as often as the day returned on which the squire had swallowed water, he not only made a point of swallowing a treble allowance of wine himself, but imposed a heavy mulct on every one of his servants who should be detected in a state of sobriety after sunset: but their conduct on these occasions was so uniformly exemplary, that no instance of the infliction of the penalty appears on record.

The squire and Mr Milestone, as we have already said, had set out immediately after breakfast to examine the capabilities of the scenery. The object that most attracted Mr Milestone's admiration was a ruined tower on a projecting point of rock, almost totally overgrown with ivy. This ivy, Mr Milestone observed, required trimming and clearing in various parts: a little pointing and polishing was also necessary for the dilapidated walls: and the whole effect would be materially increased by a plantation of spruce fir, interspersed with cypress and juniper, the present rugged and broken ascent from the land side being first converted into a beautiful slope, which might be easily effected by blowing up a part of the rock with gunpowder, laying on a quantity of fine mould, and covering the whole with an elegant stratum of turf.

Squire Headlong caught with avidity at this suggestion; and, as he had always a store of gunpowder in the house, for the accommodation of himself and his shooting visitors, and for the supply of a small battery of cannon, which he kept for his private amusement, he insisted on commencing operations immediately. Accordingly, he bounded back to the house, and very speedily returned, accompanied by the little butler, and half a dozen servants and labourers, with pickaxes and gunpowder, a hanging stove and a poker, together with a basket of cold meat and two or three bottles of Madeira: for the Squire thought, with many others, that a copious supply of provision is a very necessary ingredient in all rural amusements.

Mr Milestone superintended the proceedings. The rock was excavated, the powder introduced, the apertures strongly blockaded with fragments of stone: a long train was laid to a spot which Mr Milestone fixed on as sufficiently remote from the possibility of harm: the Squire seized the poker, and, after flourishing it in the air with a degree of dexterity which induced the rest of the party to leave him in solitary possession of an extensive circumference, applied the end of it to the train; and the rapidly communicated ignition ran hissing along the surface of the soil.

At this critical moment, Mr Cranium and Mr Panscope appeared at the top of the tower, which, unseeing and unseen, they had ascended on the opposite side to that where the Squire and Mr Milestone were conducting their operations. Their sudden appearance a little dismayed the Squire, who, however, comforted himself with the reflection, that the tower was perfectly safe, or at least was intended to be so, and that his friends were in no probable danger but of a knock on the head from a flying fragment of stone.

The succession of these thoughts in the mind of the Squire was commensurate in rapidity to the progress of the ignition, which having reached its extremity, the explosion took place, and the shattered rock was hurled into the air in the midst of fire and smoke.

Mr Milestone had properly calculated the force of the explosion; for the tower remained untouched: but the Squire, in his consolatory reflections, had omitted the consideration of the influence of sudden fear, which had so violent an effect on Mr Cranium, who was just commencing a speech concerning the very fine prospect from the top of the tower, that, cutting short the thread of his observations, he bounded, under the elastic influence of terror, several feet into the air. His ascent being unluckily a little out of the perpendicular, he descended with a proportionate curve from the apex of his projection, and alighted not on the wall of the tower, but in an ivy-bush by its side, which, giving way beneath him, transferred him to a tuft of hazel at its base, which, after upholding him an instant, consigned him to the boughs of an ash that had rooted itself in a fissure about half way down the rock, which finally transmitted him to the waters below.

Squire Headlong anxiously watched the tower as the smoke which at first enveloped it rolled away; but when this shadowy curtain was withdrawn, and Mr Panscope was discovered, solus, in a tragical attitude, his apprehensions became boundless, and he concluded that the unlucky collision of a flying fragment of rock had indeed emancipated the spirit of the craniologist from its terrestrial bondage.

Mr Escot had considerably outstripped his companions, and arrived at the scene of the disaster just as Mr Cranium, being utterly destitute of natatorial skill, was in imminent danger of final submersion. The deteriorationist, who had cultivated this valuable art with great success, immediately plunged in to his assistance, and brought him alive and in safety to a shelving part of the shore. Their landing was hailed with a view-holla from the delighted Squire, who, shaking them both heartily by the hand, and making ten thousand lame apologies to Mr Cranium, concluded by asking, in a pathetic tone, How much water he had swallowed? and without waiting for his answer, filled a large tumbler with Madeira, and insisted on his tossing it off, which was no sooner said than done. Mr Jenkison and Mr Foster now made their appearance. Mr Panscope descended the tower, which he vowed never again to approach within a quarter of a mile. The tumbler of Madeira was replenished, and handed round to recruit the spirits of the party, which now began to move towards Headlong Hall, the Squire capering for joy in the van, and the little fat butler waddling in the rear.

The Squire took care that Mr Cranium should be seated next to him at dinner, and plied him so hard with Madeira to prevent him, as he said, from taking cold, that long before the ladies sent in their summons to coffee, every organ in his brain was in a complete state of revolution, and the Squire was under the necessity of ringing for three or four servants to carry him to bed, observing, with a smile of great satisfaction, that he was in a very excellent way for escaping any ill consequences that might have resulted from his accident.

The beautiful Cephalis, being thus freed from his surveillance, was enabled, during the course of the evening, to develop to his preserver the full extent of her gratitude.

Chapter IX

The Sexton

Mr Escot passed a sleepless night, the ordinary effect of love, according to some amatory poets, who seem to have composed their whining ditties for the benevolent purpose of bestowing on others that gentle slumber of which they so pathetically lament the privation. The deteriorationist entered into a profound moral soliloquy, in which he first examined whether a philosopher ought to be in love? Having decided this point affirmatively against Plato and Lucretius, he next examined, whether that passion ought to have the effect of keeping a philosopher awake? Having decided this negatively, he resolved to go to sleep immediately: not being able to accomplish this to his satisfaction, he tossed and tumbled, like Achilles or Orlando, first on one side, then on the other; repeated to himself several hundred lines of poetry; counted a thousand; began again, and counted another thousand: in vain: the beautiful Cephalis was the predominant image in all his soliloquies, in all his repetitions: even in the numerical process from which he sought relief, he did but associate the idea of number with that of his dear tormentor, till she appeared to his mind's eye in a thousand similitudes, distinct, not different. These thousand images, indeed, were but one; and yet the one was a thousand, a sort of uni-multiplex phantasma, which will be very intelligible to some understandings.

He arose with the first peep of day, and sallied forth to enjoy the balmy breeze of morning, which any but a lover might have thought too cool; for it was an intense frost, the sun had not risen, and the wind was rather fresh from north-east and by north. But a lover, who, like Ladurlad in the Curse of Kehama, always has, or at least is supposed to have, "a fire in his heart and a fire in his brain," feels a wintry breeze from N.E. and by N. steal over his cheek like the south over a bank of violets; therefore, on walked the philosopher, with his coat unbuttoned and his hat in his hand, careless of whither he went, till he found himself near the enclosure of a little mountain chapel. Passing through the wicket, and stepping over two or three graves, he stood on a rustic tombstone, and peeped through the chapel window, examining the interior with as much curiosity as if he had "forgotten what the inside of a church was made of," which, it is rather to be feared, was the case. Before him and beneath him were the font, the altar, and the grave; which gave rise to a train of moral reflections on the three great epochs in the course of the featherless biped, birth, marriage, and death. The middle stage of the process arrested his attention; and his imagination placed before him several figures, which he thought, with the addition of his own, would make a very picturesque group; the beautiful Cephalis, "arrayed in her bridal apparel of white;" her friend Caprioletta officiating as bridemaid; Mr Cranium giving her away; and, last, not least, the Reverend Doctor Gaster, intoning the marriage ceremony with the regular orthodox allowance of nasal recitative. Whilst he was feasting his eyes on this imaginary picture, the demon of mistrust insinuated himself into the storehouse of his conceptions, and, removing his figure from the group, substituted that of Mr Panscope, which gave such a violent shock to his feelings, that he suddenly exclaimed, with an extraordinary elevation of voice, Oimoi kakodaimon, kai tris kakodaimon, kai tetrakis, kai pentakis, kai dodekakis, kai muriakis![9.1] to the great terror of the sexton, who was just entering the churchyard, and, not knowing from whence the voice proceeded, pensa que fut un diableteau. The sight of the philosopher dispelled his apprehensions, when, growing suddenly valiant, he immediately addressed him:

"Cot pless your honour, I should n't have thought of meeting any pody here at this time of the morning, except, look you, it was the tevil, who, to pe sure, toes not often come upon consecrated cround, put for all that, I think I have seen him now and then, in former tays, when old Nanny Llwyd of Llyn-isa was living, Cot teliver us! a terriple old witch to pe sure she was, I tid n't much like tigging her crave, put I prought two cocks with me, the tevil hates cocks, and tied them py the leg on two tombstones, and I tug, and the cocks crowed, and the tevil kept at a tistance. To pe sure now, if I had n't peen very prave py nature, as I ought to pe truly, for my father was Owen Ap-Llwyd Ap-Gryffydd Ap-Shenkin Ap-Williams Ap-Thomas Ap-Morgan Ap-Parry Ap-Evan Ap-Rhys, a coot preacher and a lover of cwrw[9.2] I should have thought just now pefore I saw your honour, that the foice I heard was the tevil's calling Nanny Llwyd, Cot pless us! to pe sure she should have been puried in the middle of the river, where the tevil can't come, as your honour fery well knows."

"I am perfectly aware of it," said Mr Escot.

"True, true," continued the sexton; "put to pe sure, Owen Thomas of Morfa-Bach will have it that one summer evening, when he went over to Cwm Cynfael in Meirionnydd, apout some cattles he wanted to puy, he saw a strange figure, pless us! with five horns! Cot save us! sitting on Hugh Llwyd's pulpit, which, your honour fery well knows, is a pig rock in the middle of the river -"

"Of course he was mistaken," said Mr Escot.

"To pe sure he was," said the sexton. "For there is no toubt put the tevil, when Owen Thomas saw him, must have peen sitting on a piece of rock in a straight line from him on the other side of the river, where he used to sit, look you, for a whole summer's tay, while Hugh Llwyd was on his pulpit, and there they used to talk across the water! for Hugh Llwyd, please your honour, never raised the tevil except when he was safe in the middle of the river, which proves that Owen Thomas, in his fright, did n't pay proper attention to the exact spot where the tevil was."

The sexton concluded his speech with an approving smile at his own sagacity, in so luminously expounding the nature of Owen Thomas's mistake.

"I perceive," said Mr Escot, "you have a very deep insight into things, and can, therefore, perhaps, facilitate the resolution of a question, concerning which, though I have little doubt on the subject, I am desirous of obtaining the most extensive and accurate information."

The sexton scratched his head, the language of Mr Escot not being to his apprehension quite so luminous as his own.

"You have been sexton here," continued Mr Escot, in the language of Hamlet, "man and boy, forty years."

The sexton turned pale. The period Mr Escot named was so nearly the true one, that he began to suspect the personage before him of being rather too familiar with Hugh Llwyd's sable visitor. Recovering himself a little, he said, "Why, thereapouts, sure enough."

"During this period, you have of course dug up many bones of the people of ancient times."

"Pones! Cot pless you, yes! pones as old as the 'orlt."

"Perhaps you can show me a few."

The sexton grinned horribly a ghastly smile. "Will you take your Pible oath you ton't want them to raise the tevil with?"

"Willingly," said Mr Escot, smiling; "I have an abstruse reason for the inquiry."

"Why, if you have an obtuse reason," said the sexton, who thought this a good opportunity to show that he could pronounce hard words as well as other people; "if you have an obtuse reason, that alters the case."

So saying he lead the way to the bone-house, from which he began to throw out various bones and skulls of more than common dimensions, and amongst them a skull of very extraordinary magnitude, which he swore by St David was the skull of Cadwallader.

"How do you know this to be his skull?" said Mr Escot.

"He was the piggest man that ever lived, and he was puried here; and this is the piggest skull I ever found: you see now -"

"Nothing can be more logical," said Mr Escot. "My good friend will you allow me to take this skull away with me?"

"St Winifred pless us!" exclaimed the sexton, "would you have me haunted py his chost for taking his plessed pones out of consecrated cround? Would you have him come in the tead of the night, and fly away with the roof of my house? Would you have all the crop of my carden come to nothing? for, look you, his epitaph says,

"He that my pones shall ill pestow, Leek in his cround shall never crow."

"You will ill bestow them," said Mr Escot, "in confounding them with those of the sons of little men, the degenerate dwarfs of later generations; you will well bestow them in giving them to me: for I will have this illustrious skull bound with a silver rim, and filled with mantling wine, with this inscription, NUNC TANDEM: signifying that that pernicious liquor has at length found its proper receptacle; for, when the wine is in, the brain is out."

Saying these words, he put a dollar into the hands of the sexton, who instantly stood spellbound by the talismanic influence of the coin, while Mr Escot walked off in triumph with the skull of Cadwallader.

Chapter X

The Skull

When Mr Escot entered the breakfast-room he found the majority of the party assembled, and the little butler very active at his station. Several of the ladies shrieked at the sight of the skull; and Miss Tenorina, starting up in great haste and terror, caused the subversion of a cup of chocolate, which a servant was handing to the Reverend Doctor Gaster, into the nape of the neck of Sir Patrick O'Prism. Sir Patrick, rising impetuously, to clap an extinguisher, as he expressed himself, on the farthing rushlight of the rascal's life, pushed over the chair of Marmaduke Milestone, Esquire, who, catching for support at the first thing that came in his way, which happened unluckily to be the corner of the table-cloth, drew it instantaneously with him to the floor, involving plates, cups and saucers, in one promiscuous ruin. But, as the principal materiel of the breakfast apparatus was on the little butler's side-table, the confusion occasioned by this accident was happily greater than the damage. Miss Tenorina was so agitated that she was obliged to retire: Miss Graziosa accompanied her through pure sisterly affection and sympathy, not without a lingering look at Sir Patrick, who likewise retired to change his coat, but was very expeditious in returning to resume his attack on the cold partridge. The broken cups were cleared away, the cloth relaid, and the array of the table restored with wonderful celerity.

Mr Escot was a little surprised at the scene of confusion which signalised his entrance; but, perfectly unconscious that it originated with the skull of Cadwallader, he advanced to seat himself at the table by the side of the beautiful Cephalis, first placing the skull in a corner, out of the reach of Mr Cranium, who sate eyeing it with lively curiosity, and after several efforts to restrain his impatience, exclaimed, "You seem to have found a rarity."

"A rarity indeed," said Mr Escot, cracking an egg as he spoke; "no less than the genuine and indubitable skull of Cadwallader."

"The skull of Cadwallader!" vociferated Mr Cranium; "O treasure of treasures!"

Mr Escot then detailed by what means he had become possessed of it, which gave birth to various remarks from the other individuals of the party: after which, rising from table, and taking the skull again in his hand,

"This skull," said he, "is the skull of a hero, palai katatethneiotos[10.1], and sufficiently demonstrates a point, concerning which I never myself entertained a doubt, that the human race is undergoing a gradual process of diminution, in length, breadth, and thickness. Observe this skull. Even the skull of our reverend friend, which is the largest and thickest in the company, is not more than half its size. The frame this skull belonged to could scarcely have been less than nine feet high. Such is the lamentable progress of degeneracy and decay. In the course of ages, a boot of the present generation would form an ample chateau for a large family of our remote posterity. The mind, too, participates in the contraction of the body. Poets and philosophers of all ages and nations have lamented this too visible process of physical and moral deterioration. 'The sons of little men', says Ossian. 'Oioi nun brotoi eisin,' says Homer: 'such men as live in these degenerate days.' 'All things,' says Virgil, 'have a retrocessive tendency, and grow worse and worse by the inevitable doom of fate.'[10.2] 'We live in the ninth age,' says Juvenal, 'an age worse than the age of iron; nature has no metal sufficiently pernicious to give a denomination to its wickedness.'[10.3] 'Our fathers,' says Horace, 'worse than our grandfathers, have given birth to us, their more vicious progeny, who, in our turn, shall become the parents of a still viler generation.'[10.4] You all know the fable of the buried Pict, who bit off the end of a pickaxe, with which sacrilegious hands were breaking open his grave, and called out with a voice like subterranean thunder, I perceive the degeneracy of your race by the smallness of your little finger! videlicet, the pickaxe. This, to be sure, is a fiction; but it shows the prevalent opinion, the feeling, the conviction, of absolute, universal, irremediable deterioration."

"I should be sorry," said Mr Foster, "that such an opinion should become universal, independently of my conviction of its fallacy. Its general admission would tend, in a great measure, to produce the very evils it appears to lament. What could be its effect, but to check the ardour of investigation, to extinguish the zeal of philanthropy, to freeze the current of enterprising hope, to bury in the torpor of scepticism and in the stagnation of despair, every better faculty of the human mind, which will necessarily become retrograde in ceasing to be progressive?"

"I am inclined to think, on the contrary," said Mr Escot, "that the deterioration of man is accelerated by his blindness, in many respects wilful blindness, to the truth of the fact itself, and to the causes which produce it; that there is no hope whatever of ameliorating his condition but in a total and radical change of the whole scheme of human life, and that the advocates of his indefinite perfectibility are in reality the greatest enemies to the practical possibility of their own system, by so strenuously labouring to impress on his attention that he is going on in a good way, while he is really in a deplorably bad one."

"I admit," said Mr Foster, "there are many things that may, and therefore will, be changed for the better."

"Not on the present system," said Mr Escot, "in which every change is for the worse."

"In matters of taste I am sure it is," said Mr Gall: "there is, in fact, no such thing as good taste left in the world."

"Oh, Mr Gall!" said Miss Philomela Poppyseed, "I thought my novel -"

"My paintings," said Sir Patrick O'Prism -

"My ode," said Mr Mac Laurel -

"My ballad," said Mr Nightshade -

"My plan for Lord Littlebrain's park," said Marmaduke Milestone, Esquire -

"My essay," said Mr Treacle -

"My sonata," said Mr Chromatic -

"My claret," said Squire Headlong -

"My lectures," said Mr Cranium -

"Vanity of vanities," said the Reverend Doctor Gaster, turning down an empty egg-shell; "all is vanity and vexation of spirit."

Chapter XI

The Anniversary

Among the dies alba creta notandos, which the beau monde of the Cambrian mountains was in the habit of remembering with the greatest pleasure, and anticipating with the most lively satisfaction, was the Christmas ball which the ancient family of the Headlongs had been accustomed to give from time immemorial. Tradition attributed the honour of its foundation to Headlong Ap-Headlong Ap-Breakneck Ap-Headlong Ap-Cataract Ap-Pistyll Ap-Rhaidr[11.1] Ap-Headlong, who lived about the time of the Trojan war. Certain it is, at least, that a grand chorus was always sung after supper in honour of this illustrious ancestor of the squire. This ball was, indeed, an aera in the lives of all the beauty and fashion of Caernarvon, Meirionnydd, and Anglesea, and, like the Greek Olympiads and the Roman consulates, served as the main pillar of memory, round which all the events of the year were suspended and entwined. Thus, in recalling to mind any circumstance imperfectly recollected, the principal point to be ascertained was, whether it had occurred in the year of the first, second, third, or fourth ball of Headlong Ap-Breakneck, or Headlong Ap-Torrent, or Headlong Ap-Hurricane; and, this being satisfactorily established, the remainder followed of course in the natural order of its ancient association.

This eventful anniversary being arrived, every chariot, coach, barouche and barouchette, landau and landaulet, chaise, curricle, buggy, whiskey, and tilbury, of the three counties, was in motion: not a horse was left idle within five miles of any gentleman's seat, from the high-mettled hunter to the heath-cropping galloway. The ferrymen of the Menai were at their stations before daybreak, taking a double allowance of rum and cwrw to strengthen them for the fatigues of the day. The ivied towers of Caernarvon, the romantic woods of Tan-y-bwlch, the heathy hills of Kernioggau, the sandy shores of Tremadoc, the mountain recesses of Bedd-Gelert, and the lonely lakes of Capel-Cerig, re-echoed to the voices of the delighted ostlers and postillions, who reaped on this happy day their wintry harvest. Landlords and landladies, waiters, chambermaids, and toll-gate keepers, roused themselves from the torpidity which the last solitary tourist, flying with the yellow leaves on the wings of the autumnal wind, had left them to enjoy till the returning spring: the bustle of August was renewed on all the mountain roads, and, in the meanwhile, Squire Headlong and his little fat butler carried most energetically into effect the lessons of the savant in the Court of Quintessence, qui par engin mirificque jectoit les maisons par les fenestres[11.2].

It was the custom for the guests to assemble at dinner on the day of the ball, and depart on the following morning after breakfast. Sleep during this interval was out of the question: the ancient harp of Cambria suspended the celebration of the noble race of Shenkin, and the songs of Hoel and Cyveilioc, to ring to the profaner but more lively modulation of Voulez vous danser, Mademoiselle? in conjunction with the symphonious scraping of fiddles, the tinkling of triangles, and the beating of tambourines. Comus and Momus were the deities of the night; and Bacchus of course was not forgotten by the male part of the assembly (with them, indeed, a ball was invariably a scene of "tipsy dance and jollity"): the servants flew about with wine and negus, and the little butler was indefatigable with his corkscrew, which is reported on one occasion to have grown so hot under the influence of perpetual friction that it actually set fire to the cork.

The company assembled. The dinner, which on this occasion was a secondary object, was despatched with uncommon celerity. When the cloth was removed, and the bottle had taken its first round, Mr Cranium stood up and addressed the company.

"Ladies and gentlemen," said he, "the golden key of mental phaenomena, which has lain buried for ages in the deepest vein of the mine of physiological research, is now, by a happy combination of practical and speculative investigations, grasped, if I may so express myself, firmly and inexcusably, in the hands of physiognomical empiricism." The Cambrian visitors listened with profound attention, not comprehending a single syllable he said, but concluding he would finish his speech by proposing the health of Squire Headlong. The gentlemen accordingly tossed off their heeltaps, and Mr Cranium proceeded: "Ardently desirous, to the extent of my feeble capacity, of disseminating as much as possible, the inexhaustible treasures to which this golden key admits the humblest votary of philosophical truth, I invite you, when you have sufficiently restored, replenished, refreshed, and exhilarated that osteosarchaematosplanchnochondroneuromuelous, or to employ a more intelligible term, osseocarnisanguineoviscericartilaginonervomedullary, compages, or shell, the body, which at once envelopes and developes that mysterious and inestimable kernel, the desiderative, determinative, ratiocinative, imaginative, inquisitive, appetitive, comparative, reminiscent, congeries of ideas and notions, simple and compound, comprised in the comprehensive denomination of mind, to take a peep with me into the mechanical arcana of the anatomico-metaphysical universe. Being not in the least dubitative of your spontaneous compliance, I proceed," added he, suddenly changing his tone, "to get everything ready in the library." Saying these words, he vanished.

The Welsh squires now imagined they had caught a glimpse of his meaning, and set him down in their minds for a sort of gentleman conjuror, who intended to amuse them before the ball with some tricks of legerdemain. Under this impression, they became very impatient to follow him, as they had made up their minds not to be drunk before supper. The ladies, too, were extremely curious to witness an exhibition which had been announced in so singular a preamble; and the squire, having previously insisted on every gentleman tossing off a half-pint bumper, adjourned the whole party to the library, where they were not a little surprised to discover Mr Cranium seated, in a pensive attitude, at a large table, decorated with a copious variety of skulls.

Some of the ladies were so much shocked at this extraordinary display, that a scene of great confusion ensued. Fans were very actively exercised, and water was strenuously called for by some of the most officious of the gentlemen; on which the little butler entered with a large allowance of liquid, which bore, indeed, the name of water, but was in reality a very powerful spirit. This was the only species of water which the little butler had ever heard called for in Headlong Hall. The mistake was not attended with any evil effects: for the fluid was no sooner applied to the lips of the fainting fair ones, than it resuscitated them with an expedition truly miraculous.

Order was at length restored; the audience took their seats, and the craniological orator held forth in the following terms:

Chapter XII

The Lecture

"Physiologists have been much puzzled to account for the varieties of moral character in men, as well as for the remarkable similarity of habit and disposition in all the individual animals of every other respective species. A few brief sentences, perspicuously worded, and scientifically arranged, will enumerate all the characteristics of a lion, or a tiger, or a wolf, or a bear, or a squirrel, or a goat, or a horse, or an ass, or a rat, or a cat, or a hog, or a dog; and whatever is physiologically predicted of any individual lion, tiger, wolf, bear, squirrel, goat, horse, ass, hog, or dog, will be found to hold true of all lions, tigers, wolves, bears, squirrels, goats, horses, asses, hogs, and dogs, whatsoever. Now, in man, the very reverse of this appears to be the case; for he has so few distinct and characteristic marks which hold true of all his species, that philosophers in all ages have found it a task of infinite difficulty to give him a definition. Hence one has defined him to be a featherless biped, a definition which is equally applicable to an unfledged fowl: another to be an animal which forms opinions, than which nothing can be more inaccurate, for a very small number of the species form opinions, and the remainder take them upon trust, without investigation or inquiry.

"Again, man has been defined to be an animal that carries a stick: an attribute which undoubtedly belongs to man only, but not to all men always; though it uniformly characterises some of the graver and more imposing varieties, such as physicians, oran-outangs, and lords in waiting.

"We cannot define man to be a reasoning animal, for we do not dispute that idiots are men; to say nothing of that very numerous description of persons who consider themselves reasoning animals, and are so denominated by the ironical courtesy of the world, who labour, nevertheless, under a very gross delusion in that essential particular.

"It appears to me that man may be correctly defined an animal, which, without any peculiar or distinguishing faculty of its own, is, as it were, a bundle or compound of faculties of other animals, by a distinct enumeration of which any individual of the species may be satisfactorily described. This is manifest, even in the ordinary language of conversation, when, in summing up, for example, the qualities of an accomplished courtier, we say he has the vanity of a peacock, the cunning of a fox, the treachery of an hyaena, the cold-heartedness of a cat, and the servility of a jackal. That this is perfectly consentaneous to scientific truth, will appear in the further progress of these observations.

"Every particular faculty of the mind has its corresponding organ in the brain. In proportion as any particular faculty or propensity acquires paramount activity in any individual, these organs develope themselves, and their development becomes externally obvious by corresponding lumps and bumps, exuberances and protuberances, on the osseous compages of the occiput and sinciput. In all animals but man, the same organ is equally developed in every individual of the species: for instance, that of migration in the swallow, that of destruction in the tiger, that of architecture in the beaver, and that of parental affection in the bear. The human brain, however, consists, as I have said, of a bundle or compound of all the faculties of all other animals; and from the greater development of one or more of these, in the infinite varieties of combination, result all the peculiarities of individual character.

"Here is the skull of a beaver, and that of Sir Christopher Wren. You observe, in both these specimens, the prodigious development of the organ of constructiveness.

"Here is the skull of a bullfinch, and that of an eminent fiddler. You may compare the organ of music.

"Here is the skull of a tiger. You observe the organ of carnage. Here is the skull of a fox. You observe the organ of plunder. Here is the skull of a peacock. You observe the organ of vanity. Here is the skull of an illustrious robber, who, after a long and triumphant process of depredation and murder, was suddenly checked in his career by means of a certain quality inherent in preparations of hemp, which, for the sake of perspicuity, I shall call suspensiveness. Here is the skull of a conqueror, who, after over-running several kingdoms, burning a number of cities, and causing the deaths of two or three millions of men, women, and children, was entombed with all the pageantry of public lamentation, and figured as the hero of several thousand odes and a round dozen of epics; while the poor highwayman was twice executed -

'At the gallows first, and after in a ballad, Sung to a villainous tune.'

"You observe, in both these skulls, the combined development of the organs of carnage, plunder, and vanity, which I have separately pointed out in the tiger, the fox, and the peacock. The greater enlargement of the organ of vanity in the hero is the only criterion by which I can distinguish them from each other. Born with the same faculties, and the same propensities, these two men were formed by nature to run the same career: the different combinations of external circumstances decided the differences of their destinies.

"Here is the skull of a Newfoundland dog. You observe the organ of benevolence, and that of attachment. Here is a human skull, in which you may observe a very striking negation of both these organs; and an equally striking development of those of destruction, cunning, avarice, and self-love. This was one of the most illustrious statesmen that ever flourished in the page of history.

"Here is the skull of a turnspit, which, after a wretched life of dirty work, was turned out of doors to die on a dunghill. I have been induced to preserve it, in consequence of its remarkable similarity to this, which belonged to a courtly poet, who having grown grey in flattering the great, was cast off in the same manner to perish by the same catastrophe."

After these, and several other illustrations, during which the skulls were handed round for the inspection of the company, Mr Cranium proceeded thus:

"It is obvious, from what I have said, that no man can hope for worldly honour or advancement, who is not placed in such a relation to external circumstances as may be consentaneous to his peculiar cerebral organs; and I would advise every parent, who has the welfare of his son at heart, to procure as extensive a collection as possible of the skulls of animals, and, before determining on the choice of a profession, to compare with the utmost nicety their bumps and protuberances with those of the skull of his son. If the development of the organ of destruction point out a similarity between the youth and the tiger, let him be brought to some profession (whether that of a butcher, a soldier, or a physician, may be regulated by circumstances) in which he may be furnished with a licence to kill: as, without such licence, the indulgence of his natural propensity may lead to the untimely rescission of his vital thread, 'with edge of penny cord and vile reproach.' If he show an analogy with the jackal, let all possible influence be used to procure him a place at court, where he will infallibly thrive. If his skull bear a marked resemblance to that of a magpie, it cannot be doubted that he will prove an admirable lawyer; and if with this advantageous conformation be combined any similitude to that of an owl, very confident hopes may be formed of his becoming a judge."

A furious flourish of music was now heard from the ball-room, the squire having secretly dispatched the little butler to order it to strike up, by way of a hint to Mr Cranium to finish his harangue. The company took the hint and adjourned tumultuously, having just understood as much of the lecture as furnished them with amusement for the ensuing twelvemonth, in feeling the skulls of all their acquaintance.

Chapter XIII

The Ball

The ball-room was adorned with great taste and elegance, under the direction of Miss Caprioletta and her friend Miss Cephalis, who were themselves its most beautiful ornaments, even though romantic Meirion, the pre-eminent in loveliness, sent many of its loveliest daughters to grace the festive scene. Numberless were the solicitations of the dazzled swains of Cambria for the honour of the two first dances with the one or the other of these fascinating friends; but little availed, on this occasion, the pedigree lineally traced from Caractacus or King Arthur; their two philosophical lovers, neither of whom could have given the least account of his great-great-grandfather, had engaged them many days before. Mr Panscope chafed and fretted like Llugwy in his bed of rocks, when the object of his adoration stood up with his rival: but he consoled himself with a lively damsel from the vale of Edeirnion, having first compelled Miss Cephalis to promise him her hand for the fourth set.

The ball was accordingly opened by Miss Caprioletta and Mr Foster, which gave rise to much speculation among the Welsh gentry, as to who this Mr Foster could be; some of the more learned among them secretly resolving to investigate most profoundly the antiquity of the name of Foster, and ascertain what right a person so denominated could have to open the most illustrious of all possible balls with the lovely Caprioletta Headlong, the only sister of Harry Headlong, Esquire, of Headlong Hall, in the Vale of Llanberris, the only surviving male representative of the antediluvian family of Headlong Ap-Rhaiader.

When the first two dances were ended, Mr Escot, who did not choose to dance with any one but his adorable Cephalis, looking round for a convenient seat, discovered Mr Jenkison in a corner by the side of the Reverend Doctor Gaster, who was keeping excellent time with his nose to the lively melody of the harp and fiddle. Mr Escot seated himself by the side of Mr Jenkison, and inquired if he took no part in the amusement of the night?

Mr Jenkison. No. The universal cheerfulness of the company induces me to rise; the trouble of such violent exercise induces me to sit still. Did I see a young lady in want of a partner, gallantry would incite me to offer myself as her devoted knight for half an hour: but, as I perceive there are enough without me, that motive is null. I have been weighing these points pro and con, and remain in statu quo.

Mr Escot. I have danced, contrary to my system, as I have done many other things since I have been here, from a motive that you will easily guess. (Mr Jenkison smiled.) I have great objections to dancing. The wild and original man is a calm and contemplative animal. The stings of natural appetite alone rouse him to action. He satisfies his hunger with roots and fruits, unvitiated by the malignant adhibition of fire, and all its diabolical processes of elixion and assation; he slakes his thirst in the mountain-stream, summisgetai tae epituchousae, and returns to his peaceful state of meditative repose.

Mr Jenkison. Like the metaphysical statue of Condillac.

Mr Escot. With all its senses and purely natural faculties developed, certainly. Imagine this tranquil and passionless being, occupied in his first meditation on the simple question of Where am I? Whence do I come? And what is the end of my existence? Then suddenly place before him a chandelier, a fiddler, and a magnificent beau in silk stockings and pumps, bounding, skipping, swinging, capering, and throwing himself into ten thousand attitudes, till his face glows with fever, and distils with perspiration: the first impulse excited in his mind by such an apparition will be that of violent fear, which, by the reiterated perception of its harmlessness, will subside into simple astonishment. Then let any genius, sufficiently powerful to impress on his mind all the terms of the communication, impart to him, that after a long process of ages, when his race shall have attained what some people think proper to denominate a very advanced stage of perfectibility, the most favoured and distinguished of the community shall meet by hundreds, to grin, and labour, and gesticulate, like the phantasma before him, from sunset to sunrise, while all nature is at rest, and that they shall consider this a happy and pleasurable mode of existence, and furnishing the most delightful of all possible contrasts to what they will call his vegetative state: would he not groan from his inmost soul for the lamentable condition of his posterity?

Mr Jenkison. I know not what your wild and original man might think of the matter in the abstract; but comparatively, I conceive, he would be better pleased with the vision of such a scene as this, than with that of a party of Indians (who would have all the advantage of being nearly as wild as himself), dancing their infernal war-dance round a midnight fire in a North American forest.

Mr Escot. Not if you should impart to him the true nature of both, by laying open to his view the springs of action in both parties.

Mr Jenkison. To do this with effect, you must make him a profound metaphysician, and thus transfer him at once from his wild and original state to a very advanced stage of intellectual progression; whether that progression be towards good or evil, I leave you and our friend Foster to settle between you.

Mr Escot. I wish to make no change in his habits and feelings, but to give him, hypothetically, so much mental illumination, as will enable him to take a clear view of two distinct stages of the deterioration of his posterity, that he may be enabled to compare them with each other, and with his own more happy condition. The Indian, dancing round the midnight fire, is very far deteriorated; but the magnificent beau, dancing to the light of chandeliers, is infinitely more so. The Indian is a hunter: he makes great use of fire, and subsists almost entirely on animal food. The malevolent passions that spring from these pernicious habits involve him in perpetual war. He is, therefore, necessitated, for his own preservation, to keep all the energies of his nature in constant activity: to this end his midnight war-dance is very powerfully subservient, and, though in itself a frightful spectacle, is at least justifiable on the iron plea of necessity.

Mr Jenkison. On the same iron plea, the modern system of dancing is more justifiable. The Indian dances to prepare himself for killing his enemy: but while the beaux and belles of our assemblies dance, they are in the very act of killing theirs, TIME! a more inveterate and formidable foe than any the Indian has to contend with; for, however completely and ingeniously killed, he is sure to rise again, "with twenty mortal murders on his crown," leading his army of blue devils, with ennui in the van, and vapours in the rear.

Mr Escot. Your observation militates on my side of the question; and it is a strong argument in favour of the Indian, that he has no such enemy to kill.

Mr Jenkison. There is certainly a great deal to be said against dancing: there is also a great deal to be said in its favour. The first side of the question I leave for the present to you: on the latter, I may venture to allege that no amusement seems more natural and more congenial to youth than this. It has the advantage of bringing young persons of both sexes together, in a manner which its publicity renders perfectly unexceptionable, enabling them to see and know each other better than, perhaps, any other mode of general association. Tete-a-tetes are dangerous things. Small family parties are too much under mutual observation. A ball-room appears to me almost the only scene uniting that degree of rational and innocent liberty of intercourse, which it is desirable to promote as much as possible between young persons, with that scrupulous attention to the delicacy and propriety of female conduct, which I consider the fundamental basis of all our most valuable social relations.

Mr Escot. There would be some plausibility in your argument, if it were not the very essence of this species of intercourse to exhibit them to each other under false colours. Here all is show, and varnish, and hypocrisy, and coquetry; they dress up their moral character for the evening at the same toilet where they manufacture their shapes and faces. Ill-temper lies buried under a studied accumulation of smiles. Envy, hatred, and malice, retreat from the countenance, to entrench themselves more deeply in the heart. Treachery lurks under the flowers of courtesy. Ignorance and folly take refuge in that unmeaning gabble which it would be profanation to call language, and which even those whom long experience in "the dreary intercourse of daily life" has screwed up to such a pitch of stoical endurance that they can listen to it by the hour, have branded with the ignominious appellation of "small talk." Small indeed! the absolute minimum of the infinitely little.

Mr Jenkison. Go on. I have said all I intended to say on the favourable side. I shall have great pleasure in hearing you balance the argument.

Mr Escot. I expect you to confess that I shall have more than balanced it. A ball-room is an epitome of all that is most worthless and unamiable in the great sphere of human life. Every petty and malignant passion is called into play. Coquetry is perpetually on the alert to captivate, caprice to mortify, and vanity to take offence. One amiable female is rendered miserable for the evening by seeing another, whom she intended to outshine, in a more attractive dress than her own; while the other omits no method of giving stings to her triumph, which she enjoys with all the secret arrogance of an oriental sultana. Another is compelled to dance with a monster she abhors. A third has set her heart on dancing with a particular partner, perhaps for the amiable motive of annoying one of her dear friends: not only he does not ask her, but she sees him dancing with that identical dear friend, whom from that moment she hates more cordially than ever. Perhaps, what is worse than all, she has set her heart on refusing some impertinent fop, who does not give her the opportunity. As to the men, the case is very nearly the same with them. To be sure, they have the privilege of making the first advances, and are, therefore, less liable to have an odious partner forced upon them; though this sometimes happens, as I know by woeful experience: but it is seldom they can procure the very partner they prefer; and when they do, the absurd necessity of changing every two dances forces them away, and leaves them only the miserable alternative of taking up with something disagreeable perhaps in itself, and at all events rendered so by contrast, or of retreating into some solitary corner, to vent their spleen on the first idle coxcomb they can find.

Mr Jenkison. I hope that is not the motive which brings you to me.

Mr Escot. Clearly not. But the most afflicting consideration of all is, that these malignant and miserable feelings are masked under that uniform disguise of pretended benevolence, that fine and delicate irony, called politeness, which gives so much ease and pliability to the mutual intercourse of civilised man, and enables him to assume the appearance of every virtue without the reality of one.[13.1]

The second set of dances was now terminated, and Mr Escot flew off to reclaim the hand of the beautiful Cephalis, with whom he figured away with surprising alacrity, and probably felt at least as happy among the chandeliers and silk stockings, at which he had just been railing, as he would have been in an American forest, making one in an Indian ring, by the light of a blazing fire, even though his hand had been locked in that of the most beautiful squaw that ever listened to the roar of Niagara.

Squire Headlong was now beset by his maiden aunt, Miss Brindle-mew Grimalkin Phoebe Tabitha Ap-Headlong, on one side, and Sir Patrick O'Prism on the other; the former insisting that he should immediately procure her a partner; the latter earnestly requesting the same interference in behalf of Miss Philomela Poppyseed. The squire thought to emancipate himself from his two petitioners by making them dance with each other; but Sir Patrick vehemently pleading a prior engagement, the squire threw his eyes around till they alighted on Mr Jenkison and the Reverend Doctor Gaster; both of whom, after waking the latter, he pressed into the service. The doctor, arising with a strange kind of guttural sound, which was half a yawn and half a groan, was handed by the officious squire to Miss Philomela, who received him with sullen dignity: she had not yet forgotten his falling asleep during the first chapter of her novel, while she was condescending to detail to him the outlines of four superlative volumes. The doctor, on his part, had most completely forgotten it; and though he thought there was something in her physiognomy rather more forbidding than usual, he gave himself no concern about the cause, and had not the least suspicion that it was at all connected with himself. Miss Brindle-mew was very well contented with Mr Jenkison, and gave him two or three ogles, accompanied by a most risible distortion of the countenance which she intended for a captivating smile. As to Mr Jenkison, it was all one to him with whom he danced, or whether he danced or not: he was therefore just as well pleased as if he had been left alone in his corner; which is probably more than could have been said of any other human being under similar circumstances.

At the end of the third set, supper was announced; and the party, pairing off like turtles, adjourned to the supper-room. The squire was now the happiest of mortal men, and the little butler the most laborious. The centre of the largest table was decorated with a model of Snowdon, surmounted with an enormous artificial leek, the leaves of angelica, and the bulb of blancmange. A little way from the summit was a tarn, or mountain-pool, supplied through concealed tubes with an inexhaustible flow of milk-punch, which, dashing in cascades down the miniature rocks, fell into the more capacious lake below, washing the mimic foundations of Headlong Hall. The reverend doctor handed Miss Philomela to the chair most conveniently situated for enjoying this interesting scene, protesting he had never before been sufficiently impressed with the magnificence of that mountain, which he now perceived to be well worthy of all the fame it had obtained.

"Now, when they had eaten and were satisfied," Squire Headlong called on Mr Chromatic for a song; who, with the assistance of his two accomplished daughters, regaled the ears of the company with the following

TERZETTO[13.2]

Grey Twilight, from her shadowy hill,

Discolours Nature's vernal bloom,
And sheds on grove, and field, and rill,
One placid tint of deepening gloom.

The sailor sighs 'mid shoreless seas,
Touched by the thought of friends afar,
As, fanned by ocean's flowing breeze,
He gazes on the western star.

The wanderer hears, in pensive dream,
The accents of the last farewell,
As, pausing by the mountain stream,
He listens to the evening bell.

This terzetto was of course much applauded; Mr Milestone observing, that he thought the figure in the last verse would have been more picturesque, if it had been represented with its arms folded and its back against a tree; or leaning on its staff, with a cockle-shell in its hat, like a pilgrim of ancient times.

Mr Chromatic professed himself astonished that a gentleman of genuine modern taste, like Mr Milestone, should consider the words of a song of any consequence whatever, seeing that they were at the best only a species of pegs, for the more convenient suspension of crotchets and quavers. This remark drew on him a very severe reprimand from Mr Mac Laurel, who said to him, "Dinna ye ken, sir, that soond is a thing utterly worthless in itsel, and only effectual in agreeable excitements, as far as it is an aicho to sense? Is there ony soond mair meeserable an' peetifu' than the scrape o' a feddle, when it does na touch ony chord i' the human sensorium? Is there ony mair divine than the deep note o' a bagpipe, when it breathes the auncient meelodies o' leeberty an' love? It is true, there are peculiar trains o' feeling an' sentiment, which parteecular combinations o' meelody are calculated to excite; an' sae far music can produce its effect without words: but it does na follow, that, when ye put words to it, it becomes a matter of indefference what they are; for a gude strain of impassioned poetry will greatly increase the effect, and a tessue o' nonsensical doggrel will destroy it a' thegither. Noo, as gude poetry can produce its effect without music, sae will gude music without poetry; and as gude music will be mair pooerfu' by itsel' than wi' bad poetry, sae will gude poetry than wi' bad music: but, when ye put gude music an' gude poetry thegither, ye produce the divinest compound o' sentimental harmony that can possibly find its way through the lug to the saul."

Mr Chromatic admitted that there was much justice in these observations, but still maintained the subserviency of poetry to music. Mr Mac Laurel as strenuously maintained the contrary; and a furious war of words was proceeding to perilous lengths, when the squire interposed his authority towards the reproduction of peace, which was forthwith concluded, and all animosities drowned in a libation of milk-punch, the Reverend Doctor Gaster officiating as high priest on the occasion.

Mr Chromatic now requested Miss Caprioletta to favour the company with an air. The young lady immediately complied, and sung the following simple

BALLAD

"O Mary, my sister, thy sorrow give o'er,
I soon shall return, girl, and leave thee no more:
But with children so fair, and a husband so kind,
I shall feel less regret when I leave thee behind.

"I have made thee a bench for the door of thy cot,
And more would I give thee, but more I have not:
Sit and think of me there, in the warm summer day,
And give me three kisses, my labour to pay."

She gave him three kisses, and forth did he fare.
And long did he wander, and no one knew where;
And long from her cottage, through sunshine and rain,
She watched his return, but he came not again.

Her children grew up, and her husband grew grey;
She sate on the bench through the long summer day:
One evening, when twilight was deep on the shore,
There came an old soldier, and stood by the door.

In English he spoke, and none knew what he said,
But her oatcake and milk on the table she spread;
Then he sate to his supper, and blithely he sung,
And she knew the dear sounds of her own native tongue:

"O rich are the feasts in the Englishman's hall,
And the wine sparkles bright in the goblets of Gaul:
But their mingled attractions I well could withstand,
For the milk and the oatcake of Meirion's dear land."

"And art thou a Welchman, old soldier?" she cried.
"Many years have I wandered," the stranger replied:
"'Twixt Danube and Thames many rivers there be,
But the bright waves of Cynfael are fairest to me.

"I felled the grey oak, ere I hastened to roam,
And I fashioned a bench for the door of my home;
And well my dear sister my labour repaid,
Who gave me three kisses when first it was made.

"In the old English soldier thy brother appears:
Here is gold in abundance, the saving of years:
Give me oatcake and milk in return for my store,
And a seat by thy side on the bench at the door."

Various other songs succeeded, which, as we are not composing a song book, we shall lay aside for the present.

An old squire, who had not missed one of these anniversaries, during more than half a century, now stood up, and filling a half-pint bumper, pronounced, with a stentorian voice, "To the immortal memory of Headlong Ap-Rhaiader, and to the health of his noble descendant and worthy representative!" This example was followed by all the gentlemen present. The harp struck up a triumphal strain; and, the old squire already mentioned, vociferating the first stave, they sang, or rather roared, the following

CHORUS

Hail to the Headlong! the Headlong Ap-Headlong!
All hail to the Headlong, the Headlong Ap-Headlong!
The Headlong Ap-Headlong Ap-Breakneck Ap-Headlong
Ap-Cataract Ap-Pistyll Ap-Rhaiader Ap-Headlong!

The bright bowl we steep in the name of the Headlong:
Let the youths pledge it deep to the Headlong Ap-Headlong,
And the rosy-lipped lasses Touch the brim as it passes,
And kiss the red tide for the Headlong Ap-Headlong!

The loud harp resounds in the hall of the Headlong:
The light step rebounds in the hall of the Headlong:
Where shall music invite us, Or beauty delight us,
If not in the hall of the Headlong Ap-Headlong?

Huzza! to the health of the Headlong Ap-Headlong!
Fill the bowl, fill in floods, to the health of the Headlong!
Till the stream ruby-glowing, On all sides o'erflowing,
Shall fall in cascades to the health of the Headlong!
The Headlong Ap-Headlong Ap-Breakneck Ap-Headlong
Ap-Cataract Ap-Pistyll Ap-Rhaiader Ap-Headlong!

Squire Headlong returned thanks with an appropriate libation, and the company re-adjourned to the ballroom, where they kept it up till sunrise, when the little butler summoned them to breakfast.

Chapter XIV

The Proposals

The chorus which celebrated the antiquity of her lineage, had been ringing all night in the ears of Miss Brindle-mew Grimalkin Phoebe Tabitha Ap-Headlong, when, taking the squire aside, while the visitors were sipping their tea and coffee, "Nephew Harry," said she, "I have been noting your behaviour, during the several stages of the ball and supper; and, though I cannot tax you with any want of gallantry, for you are a very gallant young man, Nephew Harry, very gallant, I wish I could say as much for everyone" (added she, throwing a spiteful look towards a distant corner, where Mr Jenkison was sitting with great nonchalance, and at the moment dipping a rusk in a cup of chocolate); "but I lament to perceive that you were at least as pleased with your lakes of milk-punch, and your bottles of Champagne and Burgundy, as with any of your delightful partners. Now, though I can readily excuse this degree of incombustibility in the descendant of a family so remarkable in all ages for personal beauty as ours, yet I lament it exceedingly, when I consider that, in conjunction with your present predilection for the easy life of a bachelor, it may possibly prove the means of causing our ancient genealogical tree, which has its roots, if I may so speak, in the foundations of the world, to terminate suddenly in a point: unless you feel yourself moved by my exhortations to follow the example of all your ancestors, by choosing yourself a fitting and suitable helpmate to immortalize the pedigree of Headlong Ap-Rhaiader."

"Egad!" said Squire Headlong, "that is very true, I'll marry directly. A good opportunity to fix on some one, now they are all here; and I'll pop the question without further ceremony."

"What think you," said the old lady, "of Miss Nanny Glen-Du, the lineal descendant of Llewelyn Ap-Yorwerth?"

"She won't do," said Squire Headlong.

"What say you, then," said the lady, "to Miss Williams, of Pontyglasrhydyrallt, the descendant of the ancient family of -?"

"I don't like her," said Squire Headlong; "and as to her ancient family, that is a matter of no consequence. I have antiquity enough for two. They are all moderns, people of yesterday, in comparison with us. What signify six or seven centuries, which are the most they can make up?"

"Why, to be sure," said the aunt, "on that view of the question, it is no consequence. What think you, then, of Miss Owen, of Nidd-y-Gygfraen? She will have six thousand a year."

"I would not have her," said Squire Headlong, "if she had fifty. I'll think of somebody presently. I should like to be married on the same day with Caprioletta."

"Caprioletta!" said Miss Brindle-mew; "without my being consulted."

"Consulted!" said the squire: "I was commissioned to tell you, but somehow or other I let it slip. However, she is going to be married to my friend Mr Foster, the philosopher."

"Oh!" said the maiden aunt, "that a daughter of our ancient family should marry a philosopher! It is enough to make the bones of all the Ap-Rhaiaders turn in their graves!"

"I happen to be more enlightened," said Squire Headlong, "than any of my ancestors were. Besides, it is Caprioletta's affair, not mine. I tell you, the matter is settled, fixed, determined; and so am I, to be married on the same day. I don't know, now I think of it, whom I can choose better than one of the daughters of my friend Chromatic."

"A Saxon!" said the aunt, turning up her nose, and was commencing a vehement remonstrance; but the squire, exclaiming "Music has charms!" flew over to Mr Chromatic, and, with a hearty slap on the shoulder, asked him "how he should like him for a son-in-law?" Mr Chromatic, rubbing his shoulder, and highly delighted with the proposal, answered, "Very much indeed:" but, proceeding to ascertain which of his daughters had captivated the squire, the squire demurred, and was unable to satisfy his curiosity. "I hope," said Mr Chromatic, "it may be Tenorina; for I imagine Graziosa has conceived a penchant for Sir Patrick O'Prism." - "Tenorina, exactly," said Squire Headlong; and became so impatient to bring the matter to a conclusion, that Mr Chromatic undertook to communicate with his daughter immediately. The young lady proved to be as ready as the squire, and the preliminaries were arranged in little more than five minutes.

Mr Chromatic's words, that he imagined his daughter Graziosa had conceived a penchant for Sir Patrick O'Prism, were not lost on the squire, who at once determined to have as many companions in the scrape as possible, and who, as soon as he could tear himself from Mrs Headlong elect, took three flying bounds across the room to the baronet, and said, "So, Sir Patrick, I find you and I are going to be married?"

"Are we?" said Sir Patrick: "then sure won't I wish you joy, and myself too? for this is the first I have heard of it."

"Well," said Squire Headlong, "I have made up my mind to it, and you must not disappoint me."

"To be sure I won't, if I can help it," said Sir Patrick; "and I am very much obliged to you for taking so much trouble off my hands. And pray, now, who is it that I am to be metamorphosing into Lady O'Prism?"

"Miss Graziosa Chromatic," said the squire.

"Och violet and vermilion!" said Sir Patrick; "though I never thought of it before, I dare say she will suit me as well as another: but then you must persuade the ould Orpheus to draw out a few notes of rather a more magical description than those he is so fond of scraping on his crazy violin."

"To be sure he shall," said the squire; and, immediately returning to Mr Chromatic, concluded the negotiation for Sir Patrick as expeditiously as he had done for himself.

The squire next addressed himself to Mr Escot: "Here are three couple of us going to throw off together, with the Reverend Doctor Gaster for whipper-in: now, I think you cannot do better than make the fourth with Miss Cephalis; and then, as my father-in-law that is to be would say, we shall compose a very harmonious octave."

"Indeed," said Mr Escot, "nothing would be more agreeable to both of us than such an arrangement: but the old gentleman, since I first knew him, has changed, like the rest of the world, very lamentably for the worse: now, we wish to bring him to reason, if possible, though we mean to dispense with his consent, if he should prove much longer refractory."

"I'll settle him," said Squire Headlong; and immediately posted up to Mr Cranium, informing him that four marriages were about to take place by way of a merry winding up of the Christmas festivities.

"Indeed!" said Mr Cranium; "and who are the parties?"

"In the first place," said the squire, "my sister and Mr Foster: in the second, Miss Graziosa Chromatic and Sir Patrick O'Prism: in the third, Miss Tenorina Chromatic and your humble servant: and in the fourth to which, by the by, your consent is wanted -"

"Oho!" said Mr Cranium.

"Your daughter," said Squire Headlong.

"And Mr Panscope?" said Mr Cranium.

"And Mr Escot," said Squire Headlong. "What would you have better? He has ten thousand virtues."

"So has Mr Panscope," said Mr Cranium; "he has ten thousand a year."

"Virtues?" said Squire Headlong.

"Pounds," said Mr Cranium.

"I have set my mind on Mr Escot," said the squire.

"I am much obliged to you," said Mr Cranium, "for dethroning me from my paternal authority."

"Who fished you out of the water?" said Squire Headlong.

"What is that to the purpose?" said Mr Cranium. "The whole process of the action was mechanical and necessary. The application of the poker necessitated the ignition of the powder: the ignition necessitated the explosion: the explosion necessitated my sudden fright, which necessitated my sudden jump, which, from a necessity equally powerful, was in a curvilinear ascent: the descent, being in a corresponding curve, and commencing at a point perpendicular to the extreme line of the edge of the tower, I was, by the necessity of gravitation, attracted, first, through the ivy, and secondly through the hazel, and thirdly through the ash, into the water beneath. The motive or impulse thus adhibited in the person of a drowning man, was as powerful on his material compages as the force of gravitation on mine; and he could no more help jumping into the water than I could help falling into it."

"All perfectly true," said Squire Headlong; "and, on the same principle, you make no distinction between the man who knocks you down and him who picks you up."

"I make this distinction," said Mr Cranium, "that I avoid the former as a machine containing a peculiar cataballitive quality, which I have found to be not consentaneous to my mode of pleasurable existence; but I attach no moral merit or demerit to either of them, as these terms are usually employed, seeing that they are equally creatures of necessity, and must act as they do from the nature of their organisation. I no more blame or praise a man for what is called vice or virtue, than I tax a tuft of hemlock with malevolence, or discover great philanthropy in a field of potatoes, seeing that the men and the plants are equally incapacitated, by their original internal organisation, and the combinations and modifications of external circumstances, from being any thing but what they are. Quod victus fateare necesse est."

"Yet you destroy the hemlock," said Squire Headlong, "and cultivate the potato; that is my way, at least."

"I do," said Mr Cranium; "because I know that the farinaceous qualities of the potato will tend to preserve the great requisites of unity and coalescence in the various constituent portions of my animal republic; and that the hemlock, if gathered by mistake for parsley, chopped up small with butter, and eaten with a boiled chicken, would necessitate a great derangement, and perhaps a total decomposition, of my corporeal mechanism."

"Very well," said the squire; "then you are necessitated to like Mr Escot better than Mr Panscope?"

"That is a non sequitur," said Mr Cranium.

"Then this is a sequitur," said the squire: "your daughter and Mr Escot are necessitated to love one another; and, unless you feel necessitated to adhibit your consent, they will feel necessitated to dispense with it; since it does appear to moral and political economists to be essentially inherent in the eternal fitness of things."

Mr Cranium fell into a profound reverie: emerging from which, he said, looking Squire Headlong full in the face, "Do you think Mr Escot would give me that skull?"

"Skull!" said Squire Headlong.

"Yes," said Mr Cranium, "the skull of Cadwallader."

"To be sure he will," said the squire.

"Ascertain the point," said Mr Cranium.

"How can you doubt it?" said the squire.

"I simply know," said Mr Cranium, "that if it were once in my possession, I would not part with it for any acquisition on earth, much less for a wife. I have had one: and, as marriage has been compared to a pill, I can very safely assert that one is a dose; and my reason for thinking that he will not part with it is, that its extraordinary magnitude tends to support his system, as much as its very marked protuberances tend to support mine; and you know his own system is of all things the dearest to every man of liberal thinking and a philosophical tendency."

The Squire flew over to Mr Escot. "I told you," said he, "I would settle him: but there is a very hard condition attached to his compliance."

"I submit to it," said Mr Escot, "be it what it may."

"Nothing less," said Squire Headlong, "than the absolute and unconditional surrender of the skull of Cadwallader."

"I resign it," said Mr Escot.

"The skull is yours," said the squire, skipping over to Mr Cranium.

"I am perfectly satisfied," said Mr Cranium.

"The lady is yours," said the squire, skipping back to Mr Escot.

"I am the happiest man alive," said Mr Escot.

"Come," said the squire, "then there is an amelioration in the state of the sensitive man."

"A slight oscillation of good in the instance of a solitary individual," answered Mr Escot, "by no means affects the solidity of my opinions concerning the general deterioration of the civilised world; which when I can be induced to contemplate with feelings of satisfaction, I doubt not but that I may be persuaded to be in love with tortures, and to think charitably of the rack[14.1]."

Saying these words, he flew off as nimbly as Squire Headlong himself, to impart the happy intelligence to his beautiful Cephalis.

Mr Cranium now walked up to Mr Panscope, to condole with him on the disappointment of their mutual hopes. Mr Panscope begged him not to distress himself on the subject, observing, that the monotonous system of female education brought every individual of the sex to so remarkable an approximation of similarity, that no wise man would suffer himself to be annoyed by a loss so easily repaired; and that there was much truth, though not much elegance, in a remark which he had heard made on a similar occasion by a post-captain of his acquaintance, "that there never was a fish taken out of the sea, but left another as good behind."

Mr Cranium replied that no two individuals having all the organs of the skull similarly developed, the universal resemblance of which Mr Panscope had spoken could not possibly exist. Mr Panscope rejoined; and a long discussion ensued, concerning the comparative influence of natural organisation and artificial education, in which the beautiful Cephalis was totally lost sight of, and which ended, as most controversies do, by each party continuing firm in his own opinion, and professing his profound astonishment at the blindness and prejudices of the other.

In the meanwhile, a great confusion had arisen at the outer doors, the departure of the ball-visitors being impeded by a circumstance which the experience of ages had discovered no means to obviate. The grooms, coachmen, and postillions, were all drunk. It was proposed that the gentlemen should officiate in their places: but the gentlemen were almost all in the same condition. This was a fearful dilemma: but a very diligent investigation brought to light a few servants and a few gentlemen not above half-seas-over; and by an equitable distribution of these rarities, the greater part of the guests were enabled to set forward, with very nearly an even chance of not having their necks broken before they reached home.

CHAPTER XV - The Conclusion

The squire and his select party of philosophers and dilettanti were again left in peaceful possession of Headlong Hall: and, as the former made a point of never losing a moment in the accomplishment of a favourite object, he did not suffer many days to elapse, before the spiritual metamorphosis of eight into four was effected by the clerical dexterity of the Reverend Doctor Gaster.

Immediately after the ceremony, the whole party dispersed, the squire having first extracted from every one of his chosen guests a positive promise to re-assemble in August, when they would be better enabled, in its most appropriate season, to form a correct judgment of Cambrian hospitality.

Mr Jenkison shook hands at parting with his two brother philosophers. "According to your respective systems," said he, "I ought to congratulate you on a change for the better, which I do most cordially: and to condole with you on a change for the worse, though, when I consider whom you have chosen, I should violate every principle of probability in doing so."

"You will do well," said Mr Foster, "to follow our example. The extensive circle of general philanthropy, which, in the present advanced stage of human nature, comprehends in its circumference the destinies of the whole species, originated, and still proceeds, from that narrower circle of domestic affection, which first set limits to the empire of selfishness, and, by purifying the passions and enlarging the affections of mankind, has given to the views of benevolence an increasing and illimitable expansion, which will finally diffuse happiness and peace over the whole surface of the world."

"The affection," said Mr Escot, "of two congenial spirits, united not by legal bondage and superstitious imposture, but by mutual confidence and reciprocal virtues, is the only counterbalancing consolation in this scene of mischief and misery. But how rarely is this the case according to the present system of marriage! So far from being a central point of expansion to the great circle of universal benevolence, it serves only to concentrate the feelings of natural sympathy in the reflected selfishness of family interest, and to substitute for the humani nihil alienum puto of youthful philanthropy, the charity begins at home of maturer years. And what accession of individual happiness is acquired by this oblivion of the general good? Luxury, despotism, and avarice have so seized and entangled nine hundred and ninety-nine out of every thousand of the human race, that the matrimonial compact, which ought to be the most easy, the most free, and the most simple of all engagements, is become the most slavish and complicated, a mere question of finance, a system of bargain, and barter, and commerce, and trick, and chicanery, and dissimulation, and fraud. Is there one instance in ten thousand, in which the buds of first affection are not most cruelly and hopelessly blasted, by avarice, or ambition, or arbitrary power? Females, condemned during the whole flower of their youth to a worse than monastic celibacy, irrevocably debarred from the hope to which their first affections pointed, will, at a certain period of life, as the natural delicacy of taste and feeling is gradually worn away by the attrition of society, become willing to take up with any coxcomb or scoundrel, whom that merciless and mercenary gang of cold-blooded slaves and assassins, called, in the ordinary prostitution of language friends, may agree in designating as a prudent choice. Young men, on the other hand, are driven by the same vile superstitions from the company of the most amiable and modest of the opposite sex, to that of those miserable victims and outcasts of a world which dares to call itself virtuous, whom that very society whose pernicious institutions first caused their aberrations, consigning them, without one tear of pity or one struggle of remorse, to penury, infamy, and disease, condemns to bear the burden of its own atrocious absurdities! Thus, the youth of one sex is consumed in slavery, disappointment, and spleen; that of the other, in frantic folly and selfish intemperance: till at length, on the necks of a couple so enfeebled, so perverted, so distempered both in body and soul, society throws the yoke of marriage: that yoke which, once rivetted on the necks of its victims, clings to them like the poisoned garments of Nessus or Medea. What can be expected from these ill-assorted yoke-fellows, but that, like two ill-tempered hounds, coupled by a tyrannical sportsman, they should drag on their indissoluble fetter, snarling and growling, and pulling in different directions? What can be expected for their wretched offspring, but sickness and suffering, premature decrepitude, and untimely death? In this, as in every other institution of civilised society, avarice, luxury, and disease constitute the TRIANGULAR HARMONY of the life of man. Avarice conducts him to the abyss of toil and crime: luxury seizes on his ill-gotten spoil; and, while he revels in her enchantments, or groans beneath her tyranny, disease bursts upon him, and sweeps him from the earth."

"Your theory," said Mr Jenkison, "forms an admirable counterpoise to your example. As far as I am attracted by the one, I am repelled by the other. Thus, the scales of my philosophical balance remain eternally equiponderant, and I see no reason to say of either of them, OICHETAI EIS AIDAO[15.1]."

NOTES

Chapter 1
[1.1] Foster, quasi Phostaer, from phaos and taereo, lucem servo, conservo, observo, custodio, one who watches over and guards the light; a sense in which the word is often used amongst us, when we speak of fostering a flame.

[1.2] Escot, quasi es skoton, in tenebras, scilicet, intuens; one who is always looking into the dark side of the question.

[1.3] Jenkison: This name may be derived from aien ex ison, semper ex aequalibus, scilicet, mensuris omnia metiens: one who from equal measures divides and distributes all things: one who from equal measures can always produce arguments on both sides of a question, with so much nicety and exactness, as to keep the said question eternally pending, and the balance of the controversy perpetually in statu quo. By an aphaeresis of the a, an elision of the second e, and an easy and natural mutation of x into k, the derivation of this name proceeds according to the strictest principles of etymology: aien ex ison, Ien ex ison Ien ek ison Ien 'k ison Ienkison Ienkison Jenkison.

[1.4] Gaster: scilicet Gastaer Venter, et praeterea nihil.

Chapter 2
[2.1] See Emmerton on the Auricula.

Chapter 3
[3.1] Mr Knight, in a note to the Landscape, having taken the liberty of laughing at a notable device of a celebrated improver, for giving greatness of character to a place, and showing an undivided extent of property, by placing the family arms on the neighbouring milestones, the improver retorted on him with a charge of misquotation, misrepresentation, and malice prepense. Mr Knight, in the preface to the second edition of his poem, quotes the improver's words: "The market-house, or other public edifice, or even a mere stone with distances, may bear the arms of the family:" and adds: "By a mere stone with distances, the author of the Landscape certainly thought he meant a milestone; but, if he did not, any other interpretation which he may think more advantageous to himself shall readily be adopted, as it will equally answer the purpose of the quotation." The improver, however, did not condescend to explain what he really meant by a mere stone with distances, though he strenuously maintained that he did not mean a milestone. His idea, therefore, stands on record, invested with all the sublimity that obscurity can confer.

[3.2] "Il est constant qu'elles se baisent de meilleur coeur, et se caressent avec plus de grace devant les hommes, fieres d'aiguiser impunement leur convoitise par l'image des faveurs qu'elles savent leur faire envier." Rousseau, Emile, liv. 5.

Chapter 4
[4.1] See Price on the Picturesque.

[4.2] See Knight on Taste, and the Edinburgh Review, No. XIV.

[4.3] Protracted banquets have been copious sources of evil.

Chapter 5
[5.1] See Lord Monboddo's Ancient Metaphysics.

[5.2] Drummond's Academical Questions.

[5.3] Homer is proved to have been a lover of wine by the praises he bestows upon it.

[5.4] A cup of wine at hand, to drink as inclination prompts.

Chapter 6
[6.1] See Knight on Taste.

[6.2] This stanza is imitated from Machiavelli's Capitolo dell' Occasione.

Chapter 7
[7.1] Fragments of a demolished world.

[7.2] Took's Diversions of Purley.

Chapter 8
[8.1] Some readers will, perhaps, recollect the Archbishop of Prague, who also was an excellent sportsman, and who,

Com' era scritto in certi suoi giornali, Ucciso avea con le sue proprie mani Un numero infinito d'animali: Cinquemila con quindici fagiani, Seimila lepri, ottantantre cignali, E per disgrazia, ancor tredici cani, &c.

Chapter 9
[9.1] Me miserable! and thrice miserable! and four times, and five times, and twelve times, and ten thousand times miserable!

[9.2] Pronounced cooroo, the Welsh word for ale.

Chapter 10
[10.1] Long since dead.

[10.2] Georg. I. 199.

[10.3] Sat. XIII. 28.

[10.4] Carm. III. 6, 46.

Chapter 11
[11.1] Pistyll, in Welch, signifies a cataract, and Rhaidr a cascade.

[11.2] Rabelais.

Chapter 13
[13.1] Rousseau, Discours sur les Sciences.

[13.2] Imitated from a passage in the Purgatorio of Dante.

Chapter 14
[14.1] Jeremy Taylor.

Chapter 15
[15.1] It descends to the shades: or, in other words, it goes to the devil.

Thomas Love Peacock – A Short Biography

Thomas Love Peacock was born on October 18th 1785 in Weymouth, Dorset.

His parents were Samuel Peacock, a glass merchant, and Sarah Love, daughter of Thomas Love a retired master of a man-of-war in the Royal Navy.

Thomas went with his mother to live with her family at Chertsey in 1791 and the following year to a school run by Joseph Harris Wicks at Englefield Green where he stayed for a further six years.

Thomas's father died in 1794 leaving only a small annuity.

It is shortly after this that Thomas wrote his first poem: an epitaph for a school friend. At thirteen he wrote another on his Midsummer Holidays. In 1798 he was withdrawn from school and became entirely self-educated.

In February 1800, Thomas was made a clerk with Ludlow Fraser Company, merchants at Throgmorton Street in the City of London. He lived at the premise's with his widowed mother.

For the country at large the new century was a time of much effort. The expansion of its empire abroad and the unsettled times nearer in Europe made for complex times.

For Thomas it was work and the nurturing of his writing. He won the eleventh prize from the Monthly Preceptor for a verse answer to the question "Is History or Biography the More Improving Study?" and contributed to "The Juvenile Library", a youth magazine.

When time allowed he would visit the Reading Room of the British Museum, studying classic literature in Greek, Latin, French, and Italian.

In 1804 and 1806 he published two volumes of poetry, The Monks of St. Mark and Palmyra.

By 1806 Peacock left his job in the city for a solitary walking tour of Scotland. In October the annuity left by his father had expired and the following year he returned to live at his mother's house at Chertsey. He was briefly engaged to Fanny Faulkner, but it was broken off through the interference of her relations.

In the autumn of 1808 he became private secretary to Sir Home Popham, commanding the fleet before Flushing and by the year-end served aboard HMS Venerable. His romantic affection for the sea was at odds though with the nautical reality.

"Writing poetry", he says, "or doing anything else that is rational, in this floating inferno, is next to a moral impossibility. I would give the world to be at home and devote the winter to the composition of a comedy".

On 29th May 1809 he set out on a two-week expedition to trace the course of the Thames from its source to Chertsey and spent two or three days staying in Oxford expanding a previously written poem into 'The Genius of the Thames'.

Peacock travelled to North Wales in January 1810 where he visited Tremadog and settled at Maentwrog in Merionethshire. At Maentwrog he was attracted to the parson's daughter Jane Gryffydh, whom he referred to as the "Caernavonshire nymph." She was to become the love of his life and they were later to marry.

Early in June 1810, the Genius of the Thames was published.

In late 1811 his mother's finances became tighter and this necessitated a move to Morven Cottage Wraysbury near Staines but within a few months problems paying tradesmen meant they had to leave.

In 1812 Peacock published another elaborate poem, The Philosophy of Melancholy, and made the acquaintance of Shelley. He wrote in his memoir of Shelley, that he "saw Shelley for the first time just before he went to Tanyrallt", whither Shelley proceeded from London in November 1812.

A circulating library run by his publisher Edward Hookham had sent The Genius of the Thames to Shelley. A letter from the poet dated 18 August 1812, extols the poetical merits of the performance and with equal exaggeration censuring what he thought the author's misguided patriotism. Despite this Peacock and Shelley became friends.

In the winter of 1813 Peacock accompanied Shelley and his first wife Harriet to Edinburgh. Peacock was very fond of Harriet, and the following year when Shelley left her for Mary Godwin he was somewhat torn. That year, 1814, Peacock published a satirical ballad, Sir Proteus which appeared under the pseudonym "P. M. O'Donovan, Esq." Shelley relied on Peacock a great deal at this time and Peacock visited almost daily throughout the winter of 1814–15 to Shelley and Mary, at their London lodgings.

In 1815 Peacock shared their voyage to the source of the Thames. "He seems", writes Charles Clairmont, Mary's stepbrother and a member of the party, "an idly-inclined man; indeed, he is professedly so in the summer; he owns he cannot apply himself to study, and thinks it more beneficial to him as a human being entirely to devote himself to the beauties of the season while they last; he was only happy while out from morning till night".

By September 1815 had settled at Great Marlow and wrote Headlong Hall in 1815. It was published the following year. With this work Peacock found the true field for his literary gift in the satiric novel.

During the winter of 1815–16 Peacock was regularly walking over to visit Shelley at Bishopgate.

In 1816 Shelley went abroad, and Peacock was asked to find them a new residence. He found them one near his home at Great Marlow. For a time he received a pension from Shelley, and was put into service to keep off the flock of people intent on becoming part of Shelley's hospitable household.

Shelley's influence upon Peacock may be traced in the latter's poem of Rhododaphne, or the Thessalian Spell (published in 1818) and Shelley wrote a eulogistic review of it.

Peacock continued to produce better works; the satirical novels Melincourt in 1817 and Nightmare Abbey published in 1818.

Shelley made his final departure for Italy and the friends' agreement for mutual correspondence produced Shelley's magnificent descriptive letters from Italy.

Peacock wrote to Shelley that "he did not find this brilliant summer," of 1818, "very favourable to intellectual exertion;" but before it was over "rivers, castles, forests, abbeys, monks, maids, kings, and banditti were all dancing before me like a masked ball." He was at this time writing his romance of Maid Marian.

At the beginning of 1819, Peacock was unexpectedly summoned to London for a period of probation with the East India Company. Peacock's test papers earned the high commendation, "Nothing superfluous and nothing wanting." On 13th January 1819, he wrote from 5 York Street, Covent Garden: "I now pass every morning at the India House, from half-past 10 to half-past 4, studying Indian affairs. My object is not yet attained, though I have little doubt but that it will be. It was not in the first instance of my own seeking, but was proposed to me. It will lead to a very sufficing provision for me in two or three years. It is not in the common routine of office, but is an employment of a very interesting and intellectual kind, connected with finance and legislation, in which it is possible to be of great service, not only to the Company, but to the millions under their dominion."

On 1ˢᵗ July 1819 Peacock slept for the first time in a house at 18 Stamford Street, Blackfriars which, "as you might expect from a Republican, he has furnished very handsomely." His mother continued to live with him.

Peacock married Jane Griffith or Gryffydh in 1820. In his "Letter to Maria Gisborne", Shelley referred to Jane as "the milk-white Snowdonian Antelope." They went on to have four children, a son Edward who was a champion rower, and three daughters.

In 1820 Peacock contributed to Ollier's Literary Pocket Book and wrote The Four Ages of Poetry, the latter of which argued that poetry's relevance was being eclipsed by science, a claim which provoked Shelley's Defence of Poetry.

The official duties of the India House delayed the completion and publication of Maid Marian, until 1822. This delay saw it taken as an imitation of Ivanhoe although it had, in fact, preceded Scott's novel. It was dramatised with great success by Planché, and translated into French and German.

Peacock's salary was now £1000 a year, and in 1823 he acquired a country residence at Lower Halliford, near Shepperton, Middlesex, constructed out of two old cottages, where he could gratify the love of the Thames.

In the winter of 1825–6 he wrote Paper Money Lyrics and other Poems "during the prevalence of an influenza to which the beautiful fabric of paper-credit is periodically subject."

Peacock added an undoubted ability in business to his skill set. His drafting of official papers was exemplary. In 1829 he began to devote attention to steam navigation, and drew up a memorandum for General Chesney's Euphrates expedition, which was praised both by Chesney and Lord Ellenborough.

In 1829 he published The Misfortunes of Elphin founded upon Welsh roots, and in 1831 Crotchet Castle, the most mature and perhaps most appreciated of his works.

Sadly two year later, in 1833, his beloved mother died and her loss naturally affected him greatly.

Peacock often appeared before parliamentary committees as the company's champion. In this role in 1834, he resisted James Silk Buckingham's claim to compensation for his expulsion from the East Indies, and in 1836, he defeated the attack of the Liverpool merchants and Cheshire manufacturers upon the Indian salt monopoly.

By 1836 his official career was crowned by his appointment as Chief Examiner of Indian Correspondence. The post was one which could only be filled by someone of sound business capacity and exceptional ability in drafting official documents.

His writing career also continued and in 1837 a 100 copies of Paper Money Lyrics and other Poems was published.

In 1839 and 1840 Peacock superintended the construction of iron steamers which rounded the Cape, and took part in the Chinese war.

In about 1852 towards the end of Peacock's service in the India office, his taste for leisure and appetite for writing returned, and he began to contribute to Fraser's Magazine in which appeared his entertaining and scholarly Horæ Dramaticæ.

Peacock retired from the India House on 29th March 1856 with a generous pension. In his retirement he seldom left Halliford and spent his life among his books, and in the garden, in which he took great pleasure, and on the River Thames.

In 1860 came the publication of his last novel; Gryll Grange. Later, that same year he added the appendix of Shelley's letters, a matter of great literary importance.

His last writings were two translations, Gl' Ingannati (The Deceived) a comedy, performed at Siena in 1861 and Ælia Lælia Crispis of which a limited edition was circulated in 1862.

His wife Jane died in 1865 and a few months later Thomas Love Peacock died at Lower Halliford, on 23rd January, 1866, from injuries sustained in a fire in attempting to save his library. He is buried in the new cemetery at Shepperton.

Thomas Love Peacock – A Concise Bibliography

Novels
Headlong Hall (1815)
Melincourt (1817)
Nightmare Abbey (1818)
Maid Marian (1822)
The Misfortunes of Elphin (1829)
Crotchet Castle (1831)
Gryll Grange (1861)

Poetry
The Monks of St. Mark (1804?)
Palmyra and other Poems (1805)
The Genius of the Thames: a Lyrical Poem (1810)
The Genius of the Thames Palmyra and other Poems (1812)
The Philosophy of Melancholy (1812)
Sir Hornbook, or Childe Launcelot's Expedition (1813)
Sir Proteus: a Satirical Ballad (1814)
The Round Table, or King Arthur's Feast (1817)
Rhododaphne: or the Thessalian Spirit (1818)
Paper Money Lyrics (1837)
The War-Song of Dinas Vawr

Essays
The Four Ages of Poetry (1820)
Recollections of Childhood: The Abbey House (1837)
Memoirs of Shelley (1858–62)

The Last Day of Windsor Forest (1887) [composed 1862]
Prospectus: Classical Education

Plays & Translations
The Three Doctors
The Dilettanti
Gl'Ingannati, or The Deceived (translated from the Italian, 1862)
Ælia Lælia Crispis (1862)

Unfinished Tales and Novels
Satyrane (c. 1816)
Calidore (c. 1816)
The Pilgrim of Provence (c. 1826)
The Lord of the Hills (c. 1835)
Julia Procula (c. 1850)
A Story Opening at Chertsey (c. 1850)
A Story of a Mansion among the Chiltern Hills (c. 1859)
Boozabowt Abbey (c. 1859)
Cotswald Chace (c. 1860)